Meant to Burn

shae ruby

Meant to Burn Copyright © 2025 by Shae Ruby

All rights reserved.

No portion of this book may be reproduced in any form, or stored in a retrieval system, or transmitted in any form or by any means, electronic, mechanical, photocopying, recording or otherwise, without written permission from the publisher. It is illegal to copy this book, post it to a website, or distribute it by any others means without permission, except for the use of brief quotations in a book review.

This book is entirely a work of fiction. The names, characters, and incidents portrayed in it are the work of the author's imagination. Any resemblance to people, living or dead, and events is entirely coincidental.

ISBN: 979-8-9927049-3-8

Cover Design and Formatting by: Quirky Circe

Cover Photographer: Cadwallader Photography, LLC

Edited by: Lunar Rose Editing Services

Meant to Burn

shae ruby

Built for Sin — *Framing Hanley*
The Apparition — *Sleep Token*
Ascensionism — *Sleep Token*
The Summoning — *Sleep Token*
Dangerous — *Sleep Token*
Emergence — *Sleep Token*

trigger warnings

Hello reader,
I write dark stories that can be disturbing to some. My books are not for the faint of heart, and my characters, many times, are not redeemable.

This book contains dark themes to include graphic sex scenes, degradation, blood play, unsafe wax play, dubious consent, homophobia, internalized homophobia, religious trauma, fasting as religious punishment, religious punishments, negative self-talk, spanking, breath play. I may be missing some triggers, so instead, consider this a blanket trigger warning.
I trust you know your triggers before proceeding and always remember to take care of your mental health.

For more things Shae Ruby, visit authorshaeruby.com

Chapter 1
Elijah

From the time I was a small child, I've been led by blind faith. It's been a collar around my throat, and the church has been controlling the leash ever since I can remember. I was born into a deeply conservative family, not just religious, but obsessed. I would go as far as to call it fanaticism. The uncompromising devotion to God, the extreme obsession to worship him blindly, it has all the makings of a cult. Of course, I'm not supposed to think that. I'm supposed to follow without questioning. I'm a sheep herded by God. And it was always meant to be this way. This is my destiny.

My father is a preacher, and from the moment I could walk, I've been taught to bow my head in submission, avoid unclean thoughts, and perceive sexual desires as impure. Demonic influence, he's always called it. Forcing me to keep my emotions in check has been my father's main goal in life, and he's probably pleased that he's achieved it so far. I've been praised for keeping quiet, for keeping my head down.

I'm seen as pure in their eyes, simply because I've learned how to act to keep them off my back. But deep down, it really is all an act.

I've starved myself of affection my entire life, and I can't deny that now...I'm famished for it. But I can't have it, and it's something I battle with every single day. I pretend though. For my sake, I paste a fake smile on my face and go on about my day. I'm admired for it—my strength, my dedication to being the most devoted I can be. By instructors, by my peers, by my family. But they don't really see who I am deep down. They've never been able to because I keep it hidden under wraps, behind punishments and whispered psalms.

My shame rules me at times, but I'm doing the best I can. And when that's not enough, I make up for it in the only way I know how. By praying the impure thoughts away, fasting for forgiveness, and complete and utter silence. Because these thoughts? They could be my damnation. I can never let anyone know I have them. It would ruin me. The church would deem me impure, my family would desert me, and I would be lost without them. Because I don't know who I am without all of this. I can't stand on my own. And so, I could never give any of this up. Which means I bow my head and pretend I'm not different.

There's terror running through my veins though, poisoning my blood. There's also understanding. That what I'm feeling is wrong, and that maybe, just maybe I'll never be right. I haven't been since I was thirteen years old when I looked at a boy for the first time. Not a quick glance, but a lingering stare. My eyes tracked movements they shouldn't have, and the first time I admitted it to myself was followed by a promise I made. To fight this, to not let it consume me. Nothing good would ever come from it. But I'm being tempted once more. Every day I'm here, in this seminary, is a struggle to not give in to my base desires. Because I know if I really wanted to, if I craved it deeply enough, Micah would give in with me. He'd change me, and I'd let him.

But I can't.

So I remind myself of the words my father always repeated to me throughout my life. That my body is a temple, and temples aren't for touching. Sometimes it works to calm me down. Mostly because the guilt and self-loathing take over and win. But sometimes, on days like today, desire wins out. It perseveres no matter how hard I work to squash it.

I wipe my sweaty hands on my pants, rubbing them over and over again on my thighs, a nervous gesture I can't seem to quit. I feel eyes on me, and I know they're Micah's. But I don't look at him. I keep my gaze trained on Father Jacob instead, who is leading noon mass. Micah, however, scoots closer to me until I can feel the heat of his body pressed to my side. Our bodies flush from shoulder to thigh. Entirely too close. If someone were to see, it would look wrong, wouldn't it? I should probably move. I know that. So why can't I? Why do I give him hope when there is none for us? It's bad enough that we share living quarters, that his dorm is next to mine. He probably hears my whimpers late at night and thinks he has a chance because I'm already tarnished. Sinful. Wrong.

But he doesn't.

I *will* persevere.

I won't give in to this, no matter what it costs me. My happiness being one of the highest prices to pay. But I don't need to be happy. I need to follow God. The devil has his clutches in me, and he's yanking me around, probably having fun. I need to make him let go. I just don't know how, and every day, it gets harder and harder to achieve it.

Micah moves his hand to the edge of his thigh, forcing it to brush against mine, fingers touching. It's indecent, but I don't move. Mostly because I don't want to draw attention to us. Definitely not because I like it. There's nothing enjoyable about another man touching me. There can't be. I tense, hoping he'll separate from me. That he'll come to his senses and move away, put a safe amount of space between us. But is any amount of space going to calm the erratic beat of my heart when he's around? Can he tell I'm battling with demons in my mind whenever he's near?

I turn my head to look at him, tearing my eyes

away from Father Jacob, and Micah smirks, giving me flirty eyes. It's obvious even to me, and his eyes dip down to my lips and stay there. I clear my throat lightly, hoping not to draw attention to myself, but also begging him to snap out of it. To look away. Not make it so apparent that he's watching me. But his eyes stayed trained on me, gliding up toward my own until we're looking into each other's souls.

Suddenly, mass is dismissed, and everyone begins to get up from the pews. We're sitting at the end, near the aisle, and Micah stands immediately and turns, giving me his back. I sigh in relief, feeling my shoulders sag as I follow behind him. Not because I want to, but because there's nowhere else to go. We still have some time before dinner at the cafeteria, and I need to spend it in my room. Alone. So I can calm down. Pray the impure thoughts away. Possibly take a cold shower.

I side-step Micah and practically speed walk to my room, but I hear footsteps following me, and I know I'm not in the clear. I'll have to face him before I shut him out, probably give him an excuse. It should be easy. I'll tell him I'm making time for a devotional. I probably need it too.

Once I make it to my dorm, I stop in front of my door, chest heaving and goosebumps forming on my skin. I turn around abruptly, almost coming face to face with him, but he doesn't take a step back. I look around, hoping no one sees what's happening, but there's no one here to witness my downfall. And that in itself is a mercy.

"W-what are you doing, Micah?" I hiss, my hands shaking at my sides. I itch to push him away, pull him in. I don't really know what I want. "Are you following me?"

"I thought we could hang out," Micah says with an easy smile, his green orbs shining with mischief. It sends a chill down my spine, the way he makes me want. "We have some time before dinner."

"Oh…I'm going to focus on my devotional for a while," I stammer nervously. But his smile just widens, as if he can see right through me.

"Perfect, me too!" He reaches behind me to turn the doorknob, putting my body flush against the door, his body right against mine. I can feel…all of him. Everything. Muscles. I need to get away from him. *Now*. Before I make a huge mistake. "We can do it together."

"Micah, I'm not feeling well." I clear my throat, pushing him back lightly. He steps away from me with a frown on his face. "I want to be alone. I'm sorry."

"Oh." He looks down at his shoes, and suddenly I feel bad for lying. "Do you need some medicine?" Micah reaches up to press the back of his hand to my forehead, clearly feeling for a fever. "You're not hot."

I might not be feverish, but I do feel ill.

"S-sorry, I really just want to lie down," I whisper, and he nods. "I hope you understand."

"Sure," he says easily, smiling again, then frowns. Before I can turn around and run away, he narrows his eyes on my face. "You have something right here." He points to below my lip, and I reach up to scrub at my face.

"Don't move." Micah licks the pad of his thumb and reaches for my face, and I go still. Not because he asked me to, but because I'm terrified. He's going to touch me. Oh, no. He already is. The brush of his thumb against the flesh of my bottom lip is almost too much for me to bear, the sensation causing sparks of a fire to ignite within me. I thought I'd doused the flames, but clearly embers were left behind. And now they're coming back to life. "Much better."

I swallow over and over, trying to keep bile down. Not because I'm disgusted by him, but because I'm horrified. Wicked thoughts fill every corner of my mind, and I breathe in deeply.

"Th-thanks," I whisper, then turn around and open my bedroom door. I don't say goodbye before I close it behind me, not even when I hear him call my name softly. And then I lock it, because it's safer this way.

My chest is heaving as I begin to tear my clothes off. It feels like hell in this room—hot, stifling, suffocating. I'm burning from the inside out. I turn off the lights and grab a match, lighting some candles, then fall to my knees. My erection is painful between my thighs, and I palm it, pushing it down, hoping it goes away. But my touch just brings pleasure, and I hiss. My eyes close, tears stinging the back of them, and one trails down my cheek. I scour my brain for psalms, but suddenly I can't remember any verses. So I do the only thing I can think of, as a last resort. I begin to chant in Latin through gritted teeth. It brings me a sense of comfort I haven't felt in a long time. There's just one small problem—my erection won't go down. It's more stubborn than I am, and it's bordering on painful.

I can't take it anymore.

I can't do it.

I sob, tears trailing down my face. "The devil touches you through desire," I whisper, whimpering. "Don't give in. Don't do it."

But before I can stop, I wrap a hand around myself and squeeze hard. I groan, feeling lightheaded. I don't think anymore, just feel. For a minute, I'm suspended in time, and all I focus on is the way my hand moves up and down as I jack myself off. I tighten my grip, doubling over from how good it feels, and go faster, rocking into my fist. It's unbearable. I almost can't take it, and just when I think about how I should stop before I die, my body begins to tremble, and I explode with a loud moan.

Cum coats my fingers, and I struggle for breath,

my entire body shaking. I don't know if it's from the force of the orgasm or from my shame, but I close my eyes and bring my fingers to my lips, sucking the salty taste of myself off them. It's the closest I'll get to what I want, and even still, I feel filthy. Corrupted. Depraved. I cry out, covering my mouth with my other hand, stifling sobs once more.

"God, please forgive me. I have defiled the temple you gave me." My voice quakes as I say softly, "Make me holy again."

I don't wait for an answer, I know there won't be one. God has probably deserted me for my sins, and unless I confess to what I've been doing behind closed doors, until I truly repent, I won't be forgiven. But I'm too ashamed to tell anyone, so I won't. Instead, I'll live with the guilt. It's going to eat me alive, I know it. Yet I know I have no other choice.

Running to the bathroom within my dorm, I wash my hands and look at myself in the mirror. My cheeks are flushed, hair sticking to my forehead with sweat. My eyes are shining for the first time since I last did this, and I can't deny that I look like myself again. Not the shell of a man I've become lately. It soothes me slightly, but not for long. It's only been a few minutes since I locked myself in my room, but I've already decided I'm going to skip dinner. As punishment for my sins, of course. It's the only way I know how to beg for forgiveness at this point.

My room is now freezing, at least it feels like it

against my heated flesh, and it raises goosebumps all over my arms and torso. I put my clothes back on and unlock the door, then go to my desk and open my journal. My personal diary. It's part of my punishment, putting my most shameful desires on paper. Even the pen is disgusted by me. But still, I write. Until my hands ache, until I feel like I can't anymore. Yet I continue, pushing through because if there's one thing I go by, it's mind over matter. And yet my mind keeps failing me.

After a while, I take a break, my wrist aching something fierce as I stare out into nothingness. My journal is open, my pen is sitting on the inked page, mocking me. Everything feels heightened. The overwhelming feelings in my chest feel like they're going to flood me until I burst like a dam, and even the tapping of the rain against the stained-glass windows is too loud. Too much. I can't bear it.

There's a knock at the door, but before I can say come in, Micah opens the door and invites himself into my space like he owns it. I know it's him—he's the only one in this seminary who would dare. Probably the only person who cares about me in a less superficial way too. I don't look at him, but I do hear him get on my bed and shuffle around.

I stiffen when I finally look over at him, and he's lying down, his face buried in my pillow as he smells it. There's a soft smile on his face when he turns my way, and I gulp. We make eye contact for one heady moment, and I can tell he senses I'm overwhelmed. He flings an arm over his eyes to make me feel more at ease, which works, and I spend the next hour ignoring him. I write again until my hand aches.

He sighs.

"You've been sitting there for an hour, Elijah." His voice makes me shiver even though it's muffled by his arm. "Are you writing a second bible?"

"You don't have to be here," I snap. "You could be sleeping in your own room—*should* be."

"And miss the drama? Not a chance." I hear the smirk in his voice, but I refuse to give in to it. Refuse to react. There's a beat of silence, and Micah continues, "Come on, what's keeping you up now?"

I sigh and close the journal halfway; my hand wedged between the pages. "Nothing."

"Lie better," he tuts, and I narrow my eyes at his face. He does it right back. "You twitch when you lie."

"Do I?" I raise an eyebrow, but it quickly turns into a frown.

"Mhm," Micah hums. "It's adorable. Tragic, but adorable."

I smirk, but turn away, warmth quickly heating my cheeks at the memory of what I did earlier. How I desecrated my body. "It's just prayers."

"It doesn't look like a prayer book to me." He rolls his eyes.

"It's…" I hesitate. "Personal."

"Everything about you is personal. That's what

makes you so dangerous. That's why I'm so intrigued by you," Micah whispers, and I stiffen. "You've been different lately, too."

"I don't know what you mean," I say softly, looking away.

"Look at me." He sighs, and I do, making eye contact with him for the millionth time today. It makes me feel twitchy, but I try to push past the uncomfortable sensation. "You know exactly what I mean. Tell me what's bothering you."

"I'm fine."

"You keep saying that like you're trying to convince yourself. But it's not true." He raises an eyebrow, but I don't reply. He sits up in bed, eyes wide. "Elijah."

I shake my head rapidly, whispering, "I don't think I'm made for silence."

"Then speak."

"I don't know how." My voice trembles as I say it, and so does my entire body.

"Yes, you do," Micah says softly, and I relax slightly. "You can talk to me. Don't keep it in forever."

My bottom lip trembles, and I trap it between my teeth. I don't miss the way Micah focuses on it, don't miss the longing in his eyes. "If I speak it, it becomes real."

"It's already real. You wouldn't be breaking if you weren't," he says, and I process that information. Apparently, I take too long because he keeps talking before I can reply. "You're not alone. Never have been."

I study him, letting the long, loaded silence linger between us. Then I speak, almost whispering, "Have you ever wanted something you were told would damn you?"

"Every. Single. Day," he replies, smiling sadly.

I almost tell him. Almost. But instead, I close my journal gently, all the way this time, hiding the page I wrote on for the past hour. "Good night, Micah."

Micah is quiet for a moment, gaze lingering on me until I feel uncomfortable. "Good night, Elijah."

The rain keeps falling against the stained glass, this time harder and louder, and Micah gets up and leaves. He shuts the door behind himself, and I exhale roughly. My bed is calling my name, and I give in, turning off the lamp on my desk, then plopping down on the mattress. I bounce slightly, then turn my face toward the wall, closing my eyes and letting sleep take me under.

I'm in the forest within the grounds of the seminary. I'm vaguely aware that this is a dream, but it feels real. I follow the dirt path up to the abandoned chapel ruins, the one I discovered a year ago on one of my runs. No one dares to enter, mostly because they don't wander that far anyway. But also because there's no roof, the pews are rotted, and there are plants everywhere. You can see how the elements have taken over the space, and while it's a mess, there's also something breathtakingly beautiful about it. Like you're standing on sacred ground. A little slice of heaven, hidden away from prying eyes. Maybe that's why I feel safe there.

I open the heavy double doors, closing them behind me, then turn around. A gasp escapes my lips at the sight in front of me, and I can't move. Can't breathe. Can't speak. I am but a vessel of heat and desire, and it feels like an earthquake is taking place within me. And that supernatural disaster? Well, it's destroying everything in its path. All my carefully curated thoughts banish from my mind the moment my eyes land on the most beautiful man I've ever seen. He looks up at me, his ashen wings expanding behind him, making him look ethereal. I must be hallucinating.

Yes, that's definitely what this is.

So, why then is he walking toward me? Why is his head cocked to the side when his bare feet touch my running shoes, as if he's curious about me too? Why is his hand reaching for my face, lightly brushing his knuckles against my cheekbone? And why, if God is merciful, is he looking at me like that? As if he wants me just as much as I crave him.

"You're worthy, Elijah," he whispers with a smile, then leans in, pressing his lips to the corner of my mouth. "Beautiful. Wanted. Cherished."

I know it's a dream.

So why does it feel so real?

I wake with a start, sitting up in bed and gasping for breath. The sheets are wet, my skin sticking to them, and I run a hand down my face in frustration. I shouldn't be thinking about him. I shouldn't be feeling desire for anyone, much less a man.

But what if this isn't the devil's doing?

What if it's love?

No, that's not possible.

I shake my head, get out of bed, and run to the toilet, kneeling over it as my stomach contracts. But no vomit comes up. I haven't eaten anything, so there's nothing to throw up anyway.

I shake my head, gulping for air, and sit back against the wall. I need to get this under control. I can't keep living this way anymore. Someone will notice. God will notice. But then why is there a tiny part of me that hopes everyone is wrong? Because if God created me in his image, then he wouldn't make me defective.

Would he?

chapter 2
elijah

I've been reeling the past few days, mind stuck on everything that happened in my room—from the mind-bending orgasm, to the conversation with Micah, to the dream that left me panting and full of yearning. I've kept my distance from my best friend ever since, and as if Father Jacob could tell that I needed a distraction, he assigned me to the library to catalogue the church's archives. I've been here for two hours now, filing my life away.

Gemma, the librarian, has been keeping an eye on me, and she's now sent me into a small room full of books from top to bottom in search of a first edition of a book I already forgot the name of. But I'm going to pretend I'm looking for it for a little while longer because she's staring at me. My skin prickles as I pretend to look for the book, fingertips brushing against spines, until one of them catches my attention. This one in particular has a peculiar spine that looks like human skin and angelic script. I retrieve it and press it to my side, hoping she hasn't seen, but when I turn back around, she's not there. Relieved, I open the book and look through it. It's written in Latin.

The pages of the book are weathered and yellowed, crisp, even. Unbendable. I crack the spine, wincing at the sound of it, and flip quickly until a drawing stops me in my tracks. It looks like the man I saw in my dream. Except this is clearly no man, but an angel. I read over it quickly, frowning. It's a prayer to Azriel, and I don't know what I'm thinking, but I tear out the page and pocket it. I'm startled by the realization of what I've done, but I can't take it back. The book is now desecrated, and it's all my fault.

I quickly shove it back into its original spot, then speed walk out of the room, breathing hard. Oh, no. What have I done? This is unforgivable. I just stole something. For the first time in my life too, and it's at seminary. Of course I'd do that. I'm dirty. Defiled. Wrong. I'm clearly capable of doing despicable things, so I shouldn't be so shocked that I could go through with something like this.

Right?

Although I'm on the verge of a mental breakdown, I take a deep breath and casually walk past Gemma's desk. She looks up in that moment and frowns, then gives me a sad smile. A knowing one. I stiffen.

"He doesn't come for free, Elijah," she says softly, brown eyes peering into me in a way I find creepy.

Like she's all-knowing. I've been discovered, and I gulp. "There's always a price to pay."

"I don't know what you're talking about," I say, walking backwards toward the library entrance.

"Don't say I didn't warn you."

I nod quickly, and with those parting words, I turn around and sprint out of the library. I don't stop running either. Everything is a blur of movement and colors as I try to put space between me and the suffocating place that's supposed to help me be a man of God. The holy place that's supposed to shape me and bend me until I break, just so they can put me back together in His image. I don't stop until I've shoved my way past the double doors of the abandoned chapel ruins, then once I realize what I'm doing, I close them and press my back to the wood, as if it will keep everyone else out.

It's midnight now, on all Hallow's Eve, and I shiver at the thought. Demons are on the loose at this hour, so I really need to hurry. I take the folded page out of my jeans pocket, properly looking at it for the first time. The text itself is damaged, words clearly redacted, others written in Latin. It's a prayer with very specific instructions, and I start walking toward the altar to get everything ready for it.

"If I say this prayer, I'll be pure again," I say to myself as I gather matches, candles, and a bible.

I look up at the sky, the full moon blinding me, stars nowhere to be found. The chapel is half collapsed. It's a miracle they haven't demolished it yet, but I'm grateful for it because it feels like my own little sanctuary. Even with vines climbing the altar and rainwater pooling in the old baptismal font, I feel at peace. At ease. Something I don't feel anywhere else. Maybe this is where God speaks to me the loudest. It has to be.

I read the paper quickly once more, then light a match, opening the bible and setting the pages on fire. I flinch, because surely I'm not desecrating a bible for no reason.

This better work.

He comes only to the untouched, the unspoken, the ones carrying a burden bigger than themselves. That's what the words on the page say, so obviously he's going to come to me. I am all of those things and more. Hope, the fleeting feeling, blooms within me like a flower being caressed by the sun. It puts a spring in my step and a smile on my face as I gather the ash on the floor and toss the destroyed bible to the side.

"Mark the hollow circle." I read under my breath. "Leave the center open so he can touch the world."

I frown, using the ash to form a circle around me and draw a symbol in the middle of it. I'm trapped within it, and I begin lighting candles around it, hoping to cast some light within this deserted space.

Grabbing the athame from the ground inside the circle, I read the words on the page over and over.

"There must be blood. Not taken in pain but given in desire."

I cut my palm, flinching at the sting and burn of it, and press the blood to the symbol I drew on the tile with the ash. Ash sticks to my skin when I lift it, and I wipe it on my pants. Then do a double-take. Because there, on the page, it says I have to bare my chest and throat as an act of submission. As an invitation. An offering.

My body is the altar.

The next step is to write the Angel's name into the tile. With blood. *My* blood. Why couldn't they just instruct me to whisper it or something? This feels vile. Like witchcraft, or something. But I still do it, recalling the angel from the other night.

Azriel.

That's the name I write within the circle, yet the one I don't dare speak.

I light the final candle, the one in the circle, and speak the truth I'm commanded to from the page of a book I never should've picked up. This is harder to do because it's the one thing I'm most afraid to admit. The one thing that will dismantle my soul. My beliefs. My carefully crafted stories.

"I am unholy," I say softly, closing my eyes. It sounds like a confession. A temptation.

With eyes closed and head thrown back, I take a deep breath and bare my throat. The room feels colder, then warmer. Warmer. Warmest. It feels like

I'm burning from the inside out. I open my eyes, and the candles begin to go out on their own, one by one, snuffing before my eyes. I tense, my breathing shallow, and look around frantically.

Mistake.

Definitely a mistake.

What in the world was I thinking?

The ash circle glows from within, pulsing like a heartbeat. My eyes widen when I see the symbols glowing beneath my skin, and I shiver at the classical music playing in the background. Music that wasn't there seconds ago. Music that I'm not even sure exists outside of the boundaries of my haunted mind.

I sense a presence in the room with me, and my temperature continues to spike until I feel feverish. But I close my eyes and tell myself everything is okay, that none of it is real. I should've never given in to my curiosity. This was clearly a bad idea—definitely not a prayer. No, this is worse, much worse. I should've stayed in my room tonight, not gone to the library. Even better, I should've listened to Gemma when she warned me not to summon him. But I didn't know that's what she meant, right? I couldn't have known and still did it. That's absurd.

If there's a price to pay, I wonder what it is. I like my soul. I want to keep it. So I definitely won't be giving it away, if that's what this Azriel wants. But it also feels like there are worse things to hand over.

My body, for example. I think I'd rather give up my soul in that scenario. Because if I give up my body, I'll never recover from it.

Someone touches the boundary of the circle behind me, and it feels like a physical caress. Fingers trailing down my spine softly, stopping at the curve of my lower back. Then a tap. I turn around slowly, taking deep breaths, and shiver. I don't dare look at the rest of him, but I do make eye contact with the brightest golden orbs I've ever seen.

"Elijah." Azriel's voice booms, and I straighten. His eyes look intense, and he sweeps them from my head to my toes. "You called me, and I have come."

I gulp, closing my eyes.

He waits me out though, and when I open them back up, he's still staring at me intently. He's towering over me, several inches taller than my five-foot-ten. He looks otherworldly, and I guess in a sense he is. Not of this world. His eyes dip down to my exposed throat, my bare chest, and linger there. He smirks softly, and my balls tighten.

No.

Please not right now.

I'm aroused and trembling, making a sticky mess inside my underwear as I ogle him. His fully naked body, erect cock heavy between his thighs, and wings that span impossibly wide. He has a golden glow about him that I can't seem to look away from, yet his wings are ashen, not white. His body is carved from stone. Biceps bulging, chest defined, and pecs thick. I can't help but focus on his small, pink nipples. I feel the heat rush to my face as my eyes trail down his torso, focusing on his six-pack and defined Adonis belt. He's what wet dreams are made of—*my* wet dreams. Which means I need to get out of here right now.

But how?

I can't just open this circle and walk away. It won't be that easy. I know it. Azriel knows it. And the way he's staring at me? It tells me everything I need to know. He's not going to let me. I'm stuck here until he lets me go.

"You can leave," I say after what feels like forever. Raising my chin, I defy him with my eyes. He understands what I'm trying to do, but his smirk turns into a full-blown grin, and I realize now that I never had a chance. He's stunning. The most beautiful being I've ever encountered, with his bright white smile and gorgeous face framed by thick curly brown hair. He looks like a Greek god.

"I don't really think you want that." He shrugs, reaching out once more, but the circle protects me. His hand trails down though, and it feels like he's physically touching me once more.

I gasp.

"You don't know what I want."

"That's why I'm here." He nods, licking his lips.

My eyes linger on the movement, and he looks at me knowingly. "To find out."

"I—" I shake my head. "I didn't really know what I was doing. I want you to leave."

"That's not how a summoning works, Little Lamb," Azriel whispers roughly. "But I think you know that."

"I know nothing," I say, voice shaking. "I knew nothing."

My cock has a heartbeat of its own at this point, and it's pressing painfully against the fly of my pants. The button is keeping me contained, yet I feel like he can see right through me.

And maybe he can.

Maybe this is how I'm banished to hell.

After all, I already damned myself a long time ago.

Chapter 3
azriel

Elijah is absolutely stunning with his ocean blue eyes and dark hair that slightly hangs over his face. He pushes it back nervously, but it bounces to the exact same spot he just moved it from. His eyes ping back and forth between mine, and I can tell he's about to lose it. Surprisingly, he keeps calm and looks at me once more. I feel his gaze on my body like a lover's caress. Slow and deliberate. Sensual. My cock is hard from seeing the longing in his eyes, and I can't deny I like how he's looking at me. It's been a while since a mortal looked at me this way, unabashedly, and the need to claim him for myself is strong. That's why he called me, isn't it? So I could take him. Mind, body, and soul. He wants anything I have to offer, even if he denies it until his dying breath.

He reminds me of my past lover, Isaac. The long-lost love of my life. But he's dead—has been for centuries—and I try not to think about him anymore. So why is this stranger dredging up memories of him? Why am I so intrigued by that fact too? It's not about looks. Isaac was blond with green eyes, and they look nothing alike. I think it's more the attitude. They seem to be similar in personality. At least Elijah's stubborn nature makes me think they are.

I watch as his bare chest heaves, the lines of his torso exposed to me along with his neck. His skin is tan, which makes his muscles look even more defined. He's fit, but it's more subtle curves and dips. As if he's carved of clay, malleable in my hands for a short time. But the showstopper? That's his face. Almond-shaped blue eyes and a delicate nose, full lips, and a cleft in his chin. High cheekbones. A sharp jawline. Dimples that are only creasing his cheeks right now because of his facial expression, though he's definitely not smiling.

He's perfect.

I want him.

I'm itching to touch him, to get in that circle and get a taste of him. His fear. His desire. *Him.* "Open the circle, Elijah," I breathe, and he shakes his head. "Let me in."

"H-how do you know my name?"

I cock my head to the side and smirk. "I know everything about you, Beloved." He flinches when I call him that, and I touch the ash with my toe. Elijah stiffens, and I know he can feel the touch on his body. "Now open the circle."

"And if I don't?"

"I don't take you to be defiant. So you'll do as I say," I reply, hands fisting at my sides with how much effort it's taking for me not to reach out again. "You'll obey me."

Elijah nods.

"Come to me," I demand.

Elijah's abdominal muscles ripple as he walks slowly toward me, his pecs tightening and revealing a tan nipple when his open shirt shifts as he moves. I swallow hard, Adam's apple bobbing as I stare openly. My eyes trail down his body once more, doing a slow perusal, and this time I focus on the bulge in his pants. He's hard for me. I can see it plain as day, and he's well-endowed. I wouldn't mind shoving his big cock down my throat if I'm being honest.

He stops at the edge of the circle and stares at me. I can feel his eyes on my face, even as I gape at his crotch a bit longer. My eyes slide back up to his, and he holds my gaze for at least a full minute, which in turn only makes me hotter. Needier. It feels like it's a million degrees in this chapel, even though there's no roof and the breeze is filtering through. But my brain doesn't seem to grasp that as a bead of sweat runs down my spine between my wings. My cock is throbbing now, and he drops his eyes to my erection and sucks in a sharp breath.

"Look what you've done now," I whisper sinfully,

gripping my cock in my fist and squeezing. "Break the circle, Elijah. Face me. Face your fears."

"I'm not scared," Elijah says defiantly, raising his chin. His voice quivers, but he doesn't back down.

"You're not." I grin. "This is much worse. You're… aroused."

"Am *not*," he breathes, but kicks the edge of the circle and moves ash and candles out of the way, letting me in.

I push him deeper into the circle once more until we're both standing in the middle together, then wrap my fingers around his neck and squeeze gently. Possessively.

"Tell me, Beloved," I purr, and Elijah swallows hard. "What truth did you give up to summon me?"

"None of your business," he spits.

"Feisty," I chuckle. "I thought men of God were supposed to be docile little creatures." His blue orbs widen as he trembles beneath my touch. "I think I'll have fun with you yet."

Elijah shakes his head repeatedly, and I slide my hand down his chest, tugging him closer by the front of his pants. "W-what are you?" he stammers.

"What do you think I am?"

"Oh, God. Are you a demon?"

I laugh. "I'm neither an angel nor a demon." His wide eyes shine with tears, and I shiver at the thought of licking them from his cheeks. "I'm fallen but not damned. Cast down not for lust, but for mercy."

"I don't really understand what that means."

"Most humans don't," I say, reaching up to brush a strand of hair away from his eyes. "I'm a Hollow Flame."

"Which means?" His voice trembles just like the rest of him, and I swear my cock has never been harder.

"I was cast out for loving a mortal."

Elijah chokes, eyes wide.

"A very long time ago, I was tasked with testing the hearts of priests, prophets, and kings. I was meant to stir temptation. I was a watcher of mortal love."

"So you made people fall in love with you…on purpose?"

"Precisely." I grin, but it falls quickly. My thumb brushes over his bottom lip, and his chest heaves. I stare at the brand on his chest—the one he hasn't seen. A sigil of a flame. "But it was me love ruined."

"How?" he whispers.

"I fell in love with a mortal man," I whisper back, and Elijah's eyes widen even more if that's possible. He tries to take a step back, but I grab the back of his neck and lower my forehead to his until we're sharing breath. "I laid with him. Touched him. Worshipped him. I loved him deeply, for years, in secret."

"A-a man?"

"Yes." I nod once, rolling my forehead over his. Elijah's breath is warm against my mouth, and I have the urge to close the distance between us. But I don't. That would be idiotic.

"What happened to him?" he asks softly, eyes connecting with mine. But I look lower, to where his lip is trapped between his teeth. It's taking all of my self-control to hold back.

To not claim him right this second.

"When the other angels found out, they erased Isaac. Scattered his soul so I could never recover it."

"That—" Elijah gulps, eyes shining with empathy. He's too good for this world. No one will ever deserve him. Only me. He was made just for me. "I'm sorry."

I pull away, frowning.

Elijah looks up at me, still trembling from head to toe. "Why are you here? What do you want from me?"

"I'm here because you wished it so." I smirk. "Because you craved me deeply."

"That's a lie."

"Is it?" I ask him softly, leaning in and nipping at his bottom lip. He whimpers for me. "You can't deceive me. I know your deepest secrets, your darkest desires. I'm here to make them all come true."

He shakes his head. "I don't want you."

"You're right. You don't want me." I step toward

him until my bare feet are touching his shoes, then pull him back into me by the back of his head. I yank his hair back, forcing him to look up at me. "You ache. For relief, for touch. You want proof that you're not broken. You called with your hunger, Little Lamb. I came as your feast."

I wrap my wings around him, and he shivers. His fingers dig into my abdomen, then fall away slowly, brushing against the hard lines and contours of my body.

"I don't know what I'm doing," Elijah whispers.

"You don't need to know," I whisper back. "You only need to feel."

My hands trail down his back until I grab handfuls of his muscular ass and pull him into me. The friction of his pants against my cock is heavenly. I grind him against me, feeling just how hard his cock is against mine, and I groan when he whimpers once more.

I kiss his throat.

"You called for me," I tell him.

"I didn't mean to."

"But you did." I bite his neck, sucking the skin between my lips roughly. "And now I will teach you what it means to be wanted."

"Oh, my f-fuuu—" Elijah whispers but doesn't dare finish his thought.

"Curse for me, Elijah." I grin, rubbing him harder against me, my cock leaking everywhere. I can feel the pre-cum, sticky and warm against my abdomen. I feel it smearing on the fabric of his pants. He'll definitely have a wet spot when this is over. "Tell me how much you *fucking* love this."

He shakes his head. "It's blasphemy..."

"Do it." I dare him. "Tell me how good I'm making you feel."

Elijah moans loudly, still shaking, and I push him down on the floor until he's lying on his back. He willingly unbuttons his pants, pushing them down his thighs, and my mouth waters with the need to taste him.

I lower myself to my knees and yank his pants and boxers all the way off, getting between his thighs. My mouth hovers over his cock when I tell him, "I know your truth, Beloved." He stiffens, cock fully erect, and I lick him once slowly, dragging it out until he cries out. "You want to be known. Possessed. Fucking used."

Elijah whimpers.

"Don't you?" I ask softly, then shift my gaze to his. He's watching me intently, face flushed, lashes fluttering. He looks beautiful. Ethereal. "Say it. Admit it or this stops."

"I—" He nods rapidly, closing his eyes and sobbing. "Use me."

"Good boy," I whisper, then take his cock in my mouth.

I take him deep, humming at the flavor of his precum. He's a trembling mess underneath me, hands buried in my hair as he undulates his hips mindlessly and pushes me down on his cock. It's the most erotic fucking thing that's ever happened to me. I suck him fervently, desperately. As if he'll slip through my fingers if I don't show him exactly what I can do for him. But I know that's not going to happen. He's mine now—and I don't let go of what's mine.

"Oh, fuck," Elijah moans loudly, and I groan as his fingers tighten even more in my hair until tears trail down my face. "Yes, yes, *yes*! I'm going to hell for this. Oh, God, please forgive me."

I pull away from his cock, parting his legs even more and kissing his balls. He shakes, back arching, seeking my mouth without words. He hasn't let go of my hair, but I'm fighting him, pulling away forcefully until my chest meets the tile of the old chapel floor. I watch in awe as his balls tighten, giving me an unobstructed view of his hole, and I take a tentative lick. Elijah mewls, his hand flying to his cock, and I smirk. He wraps a hand around it, seemingly without noticing, and I lick him again. This time more firmly.

I hum against his ass, face buried between his cheeks. "I'm going to stuff my tongue in your tight little hole, Elijah, and you're going to touch your cock for me. When I come back up, you're going to feed me your cum."

"Yes, *yes*," Elijah chokes out when I thrust my

entire tongue in his ass. "I'll stuff my cum down your throat!"

Elijah moans loudly as I thrust in and out of his ass, and I feel him softening for me. His hole is pliable now, relaxed. I'm able to fit my entire tongue inside of him; he's finally opening. His hand is working his cock quickly, and I stare at him, absolutely transfixed. The contours of his body are perfect under the moonlight, and I watch his abs contract and his veins bulge as he gets closer to the finish line.

"I'm close," he gasps. "I'm g-gonna—"

I move quickly, kneeling between his parted thighs and taking his cock back in my mouth. I bob my head up and down a few times, taking him all the way to the back of my throat, and swallowing. He's big and thick, and I gag on him, but it doesn't matter. I want this. I want him.

Elijah grabs my head with both hands and lifts his hips, fucking my throat with wild abandon. I let him control the pace, let him use me. He doesn't even know he's doing it, doesn't know how gorgeous he looks while he loses his mind.

The first drop of cum on my tongue makes my eyes roll to the back of my head, but I force myself to snap out of it because I want to watch him. I want to see him unravel. I don't want to miss a single second. His flavor explodes in my mouth, and I swallow greedily, over and over again, until his cock softens in my mouth. Only then do I pull away from him.

It feels like I could come with one stroke at this point, and I know I probably can. I'm so keyed up I probably won't be able to hold back. It's his fault. He's everything I've been missing. What I didn't know I needed.

I climb on top of him, knees on either side of his waist, as I grab my cock and begin to jerk it frantically. A shiver runs down my spine the closer I get to my climax, and my hand tightens as I begin to shake uncontrollably. My body hasn't reacted this way to an orgasm in fucking centuries. Never, if I'm being honest with myself.

I moan loudly, staring at Elijah's face. His eyes are wide, and he looks feral. His hands grip my hips as I get closer to him, and he digs his blunt fingernails into me. "Open your mouth, Elijah. Show me your tongue."

He nods and opens his mouth, sticking his tongue out. His eyes stay connected to mine, the blue in them dilating even more until they look nearly black. My balls tighten as I feel my impending orgasm, and I aim my cock at his mouth.

"Want me to soak you, Little Lamb?" I ask him, and his eyes roll back in his head. "Answer me," I growl through gritted teeth.

Elijah nods frantically, whispering, "Yes, *please*."

I come with a growl, aiming my cock at his face

and mouth. His lips and tongue are coated in my cum, and so are his cheeks and chin. He closes his mouth and swallows, and it's so hot my cock rallies for another round. Fuck, I'll never recover from this. I need to taste him.

Need to—

I crash my lips to his, sucking his bottom one into my mouth. My flavor explodes on my taste buds, and I shove my tongue into his mouth. He's greedy. Hands gripping everything they can reach: my back, my waist, my ass. Elijah has lost all control, and I hope he never regains it.

Pulling away, I lick his chin and cheeks, gathering my cum from his skin to shove it back into his mouth with a filthy kiss. He groans at the taste, and I feel like I'm ascending.

He was wrong all along.

He's not unholy.

Elijah is the very opposite.

If he's not careful, he'll become the new god I worship.

The only one.

Chapter 4
Elijah

My head has been pounding for the past twenty-four hours. Or maybe it's shame making my head hurt. I haven't been able to stop thinking about what happened in the abandoned chapel with the one who must not be named. If I even think of his name, he might appear. I can't take that chance. So I've forced myself to block that out, but I can't unsee him sucking my cock. I can't unfeel it. It would be easier to put this all behind me and forget it ever happened. *That* would be the safest option, at least. But I can't deny that he woke a beast inside of me. If I thought I craved touch before him, I was sorely mistaken.

Now I *need* it.

Have to have it no matter the cost.

When I tore that page out of the book, not once did it cross my mind that I was summoning some type of fallen angel. At least I don't think I was fully aware. I firmly believe I wouldn't have gone through with it had I actually known.

I can still taste his cum in my mouth, can still feel it rolling down my throat as I swallowed it down greedily. As if I couldn't get enough—and I couldn't. I was hungry for more. Starving, really. And when he shoved his tongue into my mouth and I tasted him again, I felt relieved. Because it wasn't a dream. I didn't conjure it all up in my head. It should've freaked me out, but that came later in the silence and darkness of my room. When I had time to sit down with my thoughts and feel defiled. Even then, I couldn't deny that I did it to myself. I was a willing participant. He's the one who coaxed me into doing it, but I don't think I would've been able to say no if I tried. Truthfully, it didn't take much to convince me.

I'm scared of what this means for me. Something inside of me has shifted, and while I've always struggled with my sexuality and remaining pure, I can't help but admit to myself that this is what I've been craving all along. Someone who isn't afraid to corrupt me, who will ignore my shame and bring out my pleasure. I'm going to hell, and I know it, now more than ever, but at the same time I can't bring myself to regret it.

That's exactly why I've been fasting for two days, as penance for my sins. If I can't even regret it, how am I supposed to beg for forgiveness? And even if I were to beg, how will I ever be forgiven, how will I actually repent, if I don't mean it? No. I can't do this to myself. Not after how hard I've worked to bury it all deeply. To not think of the impurities that plague my mind on a daily basis.

I should be at confession right now, telling Father Jacob I've fornicated with a man. But I can't. I'm too scared. I know they'll kick me out of the church. Purity is sacred here, and they'll deem me dirty, more than I already do. I don't think I'll ever be able to admit it out loud, if I'm being honest with myself. The mere thought of being abandoned, left without a sense of community, is enough to make me spiral. I've relied on the church for so long that I don't know if I'm even capable of living without it. I think that's why I've refused to leave. Why I stuff it all down and pretend I'm okay, when I know no part of me is. But there's nothing I can do about it, so I might as well suck it up and get it together. I can't think about him anymore—it's not good for me. It'll only bring me more despair.

The sense of loss I feel is insurmountable. Like something sacred has been ripped from my grasp. And maybe that's exactly what's happening—but I'll never be able to do anything about it. This is a choice I have to make for myself. Because the alternative, living in sin, is not a life I could ever lead. Not for long. It's not sustainable.

So I won't.

With that decided, I sigh and look up from my bible. My hand is cramping from how much I've written in my notebook. Bible study is in full swing, and all my friends are laser-focused, everyone but Micah. No, he's staring at me intently, clearly trying to read me. There's a smirk on his lips, and I quickly look away from him. I really don't need any more temptation in my life. I have to push him away too. It's the only way I'll be safe from this feeling festering inside of me. Like I'm rotting with yearning from the inside out, and there's nothing I can do to make it stop. But I have to try. That much I do know.

This time, though, I don't feel excitement when he looks at me. It almost feels wrong. Like when you put on the wrong size shoe. Uncomfortable. It's because he's not right any longer. The only one I want looking at me like that is the fallen angel plaguing my thoughts, invading them as if he owns my mind. He's living rent-free in my head, and I can't seem to evict him. I also don't have the will to. Because if I can never do it again, if I can't ever experience him again, at least I'll have my thoughts to get me through the rest of my life.

At least I can say I experienced it.

Someone who only had eyes for me. Who was obsessed, even if for only a few minutes. Someone who was clearly enjoying himself when he had my body at his mercy.

I'll be honest though. No amount of purity devotionals or begging for forgiveness will erase his imprint from my body. He's stuck there, for better or worse. And in that moment? When he was touching me as if I was holy and not at all tainted? I wanted so much more than what he gave me. I hate myself for even thinking it, but I wanted him inside me. I wanted him to truly claim me. I wanted him to possess me. To own me.

Even if that meant God striking me down.

It would've been well worth it.

Clearing my throat, Brother Jonah looks up at me from his bible. His eyes are inquisitive as I gather my belongings and stand. Micah raises an eyebrow but stays silent, waiting for me to speak too. I smile tightly, looking away from him because I don't know what I'm doing anymore. Just a few days ago, I would've given anything to sin with him; now I can't see myself with him at all.

"I need a bath," I say softly, and Micah's eyes roam down my body, a slow perusal, then back up. They focus on my lips, and I shift from one foot to the other and look away. "Then I'm going to bed."

"I'll walk you," Micah offers, starting to push away from the table, about to stand up.

I clear my throat and quickly shake my head. "No, no. I'm good." I try to give him a reassuring smile, but I'm pretty sure I just look constipated. I don't want to be in close quarters with him right now though. I feel vulnerable. Even if I don't want to act on anything with him right now, I just might. I feel desperate enough to feel what I did the other night. However, I'm sure he's not as skilled as my—

My *what?*

Nothing, that's what.

Azriel isn't anything of mine.

"A-are you sure?" Micah stutters, visibly flustered that I've shot him down.

"Yes." I nod once. "Don't let me distract you from God, Micah." I smile softly, then turn on my heel and walk away. But not before I see the confusion and pain on his face. I feel guilty about a lot already, and I'm not sticking around long enough to add this to the pile too.

I practically speed walk through the building, passing the cafeteria and the library, headed for the living quarters. There's a communal kitchen and living room that are in the same area, an open floor plan that spans a pretty spacious square footage. Right behind the sectional couch, there's a long hallway with bedrooms. I practically run to mine, shutting the door and locking it. I don't want any interruptions right now, and even though I know I'm going to regret it later, I can't seem to stop myself as I set my belongings on the floor beside my desk and begin to strip.

My clothes are flying everywhere, half-haphazardly. I don't bother slowing down or caring about where anything lands. I toe off my shoes and open my bathroom door, thanking my lucky stars that it's a private one. I take a deep breath and turn the faucet, letting hot water fill the tub. Not scalding, but barely comfortable. Once full, I get in and turn it off.

I rest my head against the wall, trying to ignore the incessant throbbing between my legs, but it's getting harder and harder to accomplish that. I close my eyes and take deep breaths, but I'm weak, and I give up quickly. My hand wraps around my cock, hard as steel, and I whimper. It almost sounds like I'm in pain, and maybe that's the most accurate way to describe my mental state at the moment. I'm doing this against every instinct of mine. I wish with every fiber of my being that I could ignore the thumping in my balls when I think of him, but I just can't take it anymore. I need relief. Maybe then I'll be able to stop thinking about everything that happened. Hopefully at least for a couple of hours. It seems he's the only thing occupying my thoughts lately.

Seems like I'm going to be a sinner for the rest of my life.

I just need to see him one more time. That's it. No more after that. I just need to experience this again and I won't ever ask for anything else. *Never* again. I swear it. God, *please* bring him back to me.

My lips part, and I shudder as I realize what I've done. Begging and pleading when I should be forcing him from my mind. But I can't help it anymore, I can't seem to stop craving him. I think I understand why addicts are considered to be ill. I definitely feel sick right now. Needing someone this much has to be an ailment, right?

My hand shifts up, then down, and I moan. My eyes are still closed, and it's like a montage of images behind my eyelids. Memories of him owning me, taking me apart, and putting me back together. The sight of his mouth wrapped around my length, taking me to the back of his throat. I've never felt anything like it, and my hand doesn't even begin to do it justice. It was so warm and oh so wet. And the taste of his cum on my tongue? I'm still savoring it even though it's long gone.

I can still remember the weight of his body on top of me, pinning me to the tile as I looked up at him with my mouth wide open and tongue out, waiting for my reward. And it sure felt like one. Like I had been such a good boy for him that he couldn't help but give himself over to me. And I wanted him so badly. Oh, God, I can't even explain how much I needed him. The way I still do.

My hand shuttles up and down on my length quickly, and I tighten my fist, hissing. Pleasure skates down my spine as the images in my mind's eye shift, turning into something even more forbidden. Something searing hot that I'm not sure I'll ever be able to handle the temperature of.

I'm suddenly bound to the altar at the abandoned chapel ruins, Azriel between my thighs. I'm spread open for him, knees pushed toward my chest, utterly vulnerable. His cock is slotted at my entrance, and when he pushes in, it's not pain I feel. No, it's so much worse. It's blinding pleasure instead. He hits something inside of me that makes me see black, and I throw my head back and moan his name.

I think it slips from my lips too as my hand quickens, and I feel my impending orgasm rush forward, pushing to the surface. It's right there—all I need to do is reach out and take it.

His mouth hovers over mine as his hand rests next to my head, and he shifts his hips, then pushes forward. My body jolts, shifting on the altar, and I tremble like a leaf. My cock is primed, set to explode, and his eyes are intense as they focus on my own. Ashen wings shift above us, and suddenly I'm being hidden from the outside world. From God's gaze. I feel cocooned in his arms, safer than I've ever been in my entire life. For the first time ever, nothing and no one exists.

Azriel sits back on his haunches, pushing my knees into my chest, drilling into me harder and faster, and my lips part as I let out garbled sounds and curses I didn't know I was capable of uttering. Without warning, he grabs my legs and spreads them wide, looking down at my cock with his bottom lip trapped between his teeth. I'm leaking, making a mess of myself, and he groans at the sight.

"Touch your pretty cock, Elijah," Azriel demands. "I want to see it explode."

And I do, wrapping a hand around myself and tugging roughly, quickly. He wraps a hand around my throat and squeezes tightly, but it only heightens the pleasure. Just as I'm about to come, he lets go of my throat and lowers his lips to mine. His tongue shoves into my mouth, and I suck on it as my spine tingles and my balls draw up. The groan he lets out has my hand's movements becoming jerky, and my ass clenches. Cum shoots out of my cock, and Azriel's hips stutter.

It's the look on his face as he comes, the one I've already witnessed in real life, that triggers my orgasm. I explode—there's no other way to describe it. Cum erupts out of me, and I open my mouth on a silent scream, trying to hold back. My throat is raw from the effort to not cry out in pleasure, but there's one thing I just can't hold back.

"*Azriel.*" His name falls from my lips, completely unbidden. A plea, a promise, a guttural sound that precedes my undoing.

I'm shaking violently, water sloshing as my back arches, and I ride out the wave crashing over me and taking me under. I can barely breathe, and I just lie there in shock, panting, as I come down from the high. It's never felt like this before, and I'm convinced it's because I was imagining *him*.

I shake my head and drain the tub, rinsing myself, then stepping out. Making quick work of drying myself, I swipe a hand over the fogged-up mirror to look at myself. Flushed cheeks, swollen lips, and hair askew. I look like an absolute mess, yet I can't be bothered. What stops me in my tracks and makes me purse my lips is the sight of the flame sigil carved into my flesh. The one marring the skin on my chest. It's been there since that fateful night at the chapel. Since he owned me, took me for himself. When I first saw it, I freaked out. Well, that's the understatement of the year. I got on my knees and prayed for hours, hoping that the proof of my defilement would disappear. But no such luck.

Now, the sight does something to me, and while I wish I was disgusted, instead I feel wanted. Claimed in a way I never thought I could be. It's wrong, and I know it. So I shake my head, trying to get the sinful thoughts out of my head, and open the door.

My room is cold as I dry off and put boxer briefs on, throwing my towel on the floor and climbing into bed. My bottom lip trembles as I stare up at the ceiling, and I feel hot tears tracking down my cheeks. But I feel light years away, completely detached from my body as I apologize to God over and over.

This isn't me.

This *can't* be me.

I have to fix this somehow.

Chapter 5
azriel

The room is bathed in darkness as I stand next to the bed where Elijah's slumbering form lies peacefully, only the soft light of the moon slipping in through the blinds. His brows are furrowed even in sleep, and I want to smooth out the line between them and reassure him. I won't though. That's not why I'm here.

He called to me earlier. I heard him, and I always answer his pleas. So here I am, standing in my human form, stark naked and ready to climb into his bed and make him mine once more. He stirs, arm outstretched and resting above his head, and I take one last look at him before pulling back the covers. There, next to him, is his underwear on the bed. He must have taken it off in his sleep, and that does something to my insides that I refuse to explore at the moment.

I want to ruin his carefully crafted facade—that's the only thing I want to focus on right now. Maybe it's cruel of me to want to do that to someone clearly struggling with his sexuality, but I never claimed to be good. I want him to admit it to himself, to me. That he can't get enough of this. That he wants this. Wants *me*.

Climbing into bed, I carefully straddle his hips and rest my knees on the bed. Then I lower myself onto his naked cock and grind my hole against him slowly. Intense pleasure wraps itself around my limbs, and I shudder. I feel him growing hard under me, and a little whimper escapes his lips. It makes my cock rock hard, and my nostrils flare as I grind a little harder. His hands fly up to my hips, fingers digging into my flesh roughly until I'm sure my skin will be bruised later. He lifts his hips and thrusts against me, and when the head of his cock pokes my hole, his eyes flutter open. Elijah's eyes widen upon seeing me, and I'm trying to decipher everything behind his gaze as if it's Morse code. I see heat. Lust. Relief. But I also see fear.

Fear that it's real.

Fear that it's not.

His eyes slam shut, and he shakes his head, reciting scripture at a pace that is barely comprehensible, begging for God to save him. I grind my ass harder on his cock, rubbing my hole against the head, and little puffs of air escape his lips as he tries to stifle his moans but is unable to.

I smirk. "God's not here to save you, Little Lamb."

His eyes open once more at my words, and I circle my hips. He bites his bottom lip. "I am."

Elijah shakes his head quickly as if trying to clear it. "I cast you out. In the name of God—"

I chuckle lowly. "Oh, spare me your false words, Beloved. Your heart is beating louder than your prayers. I can practically taste the desire thrumming through your veins."

"Please leave," he whispers. "This place is holy."

I laugh low and slow, and he shivers. "Is it? You dream of me, Elijah. Every time you touch yourself in the dark, it's my name in the back of your throat."

"That's a lie," he says gruffly, tensing. "I would never—"

"Lie to God if you have to, but don't insult me," I snarl. "I know what lives behind your eyes when you close them at night. *Me*."

Elijah is silent.

"If you could take what you want, no guilt, no penance, no witness. Would you take it, Little Lamb?"

"I don't know," he whispers, barely audible.

"You do," I affirm. "You don't want salvation, Elijah. You want to feel something," I whisper back, leaning in. I want to expose him, peel back his flesh and take a long, hard look. "I know you ache deep down. For something warm. Something real. You ache for *me*."

"This isn't who I am."

"Isn't it?" I taunt. "Your body betrays your prayers,

Beloved. If you're not careful, God will see your deceit."

I shift my face and bite his neck, then lick a trail down to his chest, lapping at the sweat droplets there. It feels like a million degrees in this room, and our hot bodies pressed together is driving me out of my mind. I shift my hips and thrust my cock against his abs, and his long fingers dig into me once more.

His chest is heaving as pants escape his lips in rapid succession, and I take his nipple between my lips and suck hard, then tug with my teeth. Elijah groans, hands flying to the back of my head and holding me in place, all but begging me to keep going. To never stop.

My suspicions are confirmed when he whimpers and says, "D-don't stop." His voice breaks. "P-p-please."

I let go of his nipple, face buried in his chest. "Please, Azriel." I kiss his warm skin. "Say it. Say my name," I tell him softly.

"P-please, Azriel," he pleads, not even hesitating.

"What do you want?" I smirk, and he lets go of my head. I lift my hips and grab his hard cock in my hand, pressing it to mine and wrapping my hand around both of us. We're both leaking pre-cum, and it's an easy glide when I grip him hard and shift my hand to jerk us both. "Name it and it's yours."

"I don't know," he admits.

"Say it, Elijah. Whisper it if you must." I press my

forehead to his, my lips brushing against his bottom one. "Admit what you crave. Do it for *you*."

"I don't want this."

"Yes, you do," I whisper, biting his bottom lip and jerking us slowly. "You're just afraid it'll feel like heaven."

Elijah moans, and my fist tightens around us as I go faster. Our chests are heaving in unison, and I can hear our quickening breaths, soft pants echoing in the silence of the room. Gasps and groans begin to escape him as I bite his jaw, then lick the skin lined with stubble. My hand trails down his chest until I reach his pec, and I squeeze. His hips lift into my grip, and he begins to rock into my fist. With mouth wide open, I watch as his eyes open and focus on mine, pupils blown out as he watches me. My fingers pinch his nipple, and he whimpers, coating my hand in more pre-cum.

He's practically convulsing from pleasure, letting me worship him thoroughly.

"Yes, Elijah," I moan. "Say how much you love this. You feel the pull beneath your ribs, don't you? The thread that tightens every time I breathe against your lips." I lean in close to his face until we're sharing breath, then bite his bottom lip and pull. He gasps. "You're unraveling for me—one whispered promise at a time."

"What do you promise me?" he moans, thrusting his cock into my fist again and again. He's feral now, unable to control himself. "Tell me," he says through gritted teeth as he begins to tremble.

"Rapture," I growl. "Freedom."

I crash my lips to his as his cock begins to throb in my grip. It pulses as he comes, and for a split second, right before I thrust my tongue into his eager mouth, he gasps my name.

"*Azriel.*"

I moan as his cum drenches my cock, making my hand slippery and wet. It feels divine, and it makes me think about what it would feel like to be in his ass. Surely it would break me, completely obliterate my mind. Because once I do it, I know I won't be able to stop myself from taking him again and again and again.

I hum as I feel the familiar tingling at the base of my spine, the delicious way my balls draw up until I can't breathe. Elijah chooses this moment to suck on my tongue, and my stomach flips as I tense. He mewls against my lips as my cock throbs against his, and I feel him soften against me. But I don't let go, and when I come, I growl his name against his hot mouth. His heavy breaths and whimpering feel forbidden in the darkness with his head thrown back in pleasure, making him look more angelic than I've ever been.

Elijah is saintly, and I'm meant to ruin him.

His eyes flutter open and look into mine, and his hands reach up and roam over my shoulders, drifting down to my back. They trace the scars where my wings should be, and his lips part when I shudder. But he doesn't stop; instead, his hands keep descending until they reach the dimples above my ass. His thumbs dip into them, and his lips quiver.

He's touching me, allowing himself to explore my body momentarily. His hands grip my hips again, squeezing once, then shifting to my ass. He kneads my cheeks in his hands, pulling them apart, then dipping his finger down my crease until he's touching my hole. My lips part at his audacity, but I don't stop him. I also don't stop the breathy moan that escapes me, though I do think I need to control the little flutter in my stomach that happens when he looks at me like this. Like I'm the center of his universe.

"Do you want me there?" he asks in a whisper, and I nod once, leaning forward to invite him in. I don't even care that his fingers are dry. I want him that badly. "Will you let me in it?"

"Yes," I groan when he taps against my rim. "Two fingers."

I can feel my cock thickening again, and when he brings his fingers to my mouth and pushes them between my lips, I feel like I'm going to crawl out of my skin. But not in a bad way. No—this is so much worse. Because I can't get enough of him, and this side of him that he doesn't show anyone else, that only I get to witness, is going to drive me absolutely wild.

Elijah presses down on my tongue and shoves his digits to the back of my throat, but I don't gag. He pulls them back slightly, and I clamp my lips over him, gathering saliva and letting it coat his fingers. When he pulls them all the way out, they're absolutely dripping.

"Yes," I whisper. "Put them in my ass, Eli. I swear you'll want to live in it from now on."

"And what happens if I do?" His voice trembles as he asks, his fingers nudging my entrance once more.

"I might just let you," I reply, gasping at the invasion of his fingers pressing against me, entering me roughly.

He's punishing in his movements, quickly breaking through the tight ring of muscle, pushing deeply until his knuckles touch my ass. It stings, but it quickly morphs into pleasure when he curls his fingers inside of me. I rock back into him, making our cocks grind together. His cock is growing beneath mine again, and I tighten my ass around his digits.

Elijah moans at the slippery wetness between us. We're still drenched in cum, our cocks slick and swollen once more. His lips part as I grind harder, making him push his fingers deeper into me, and he continues to hit my prostate with every curl. The sounds coming out of me are unlike anything I've ever heard from myself before. I'm turning into a slutty mess for him.

Me.

Oh, fuck.

This isn't good.

His touch is rough, the curl of his fingers unforgiving. He grabs my jaw and pulls me down toward him, crashing his mouth to mine. I lose myself in him, rocking faster, thighs clamped tightly around his hips as he fucks my hole with his fingers. I can't explain the hurricane of feelings taking place inside my chest, but I can say with certainty I've never felt like this before. Like I could give myself over to him.

I've only ever bottomed for one other person, and it's been centuries since I did it. I never in my wildest dreams could've imagined I'd want to do it again. I swore to myself I wouldn't. But with him? Everything feels natural, even the way I bloom for him like a pretty little flower. He's not dominant in the slightest, and yet I'm submitting anyway. And Elijah? He's eating it up, not missing a step. Not a single one.

Elijah's fingers graze over my prostate, lighting me up from the inside out, and I lose it. "Y-yes, yes, *please*, right there," I mewl. "Don't stop. Fuck me, Eli. Harder, please."

He pumps his fingers in and out faster and harder, curling them against my prostate, and moans when I grind against him harder, putting all my body weight on him. I tilt my hips, arching my back and pushing my ass back against his fingers, trying to give him even better access. Trying to give him everything. Every single part of me is on the line right now, and I don't know how to hold myself back.

"Az," Elijah says through gritted teeth, and my stomach flips at the nickname. I'm dancing on the edge of a cliff, and I just need one more little push to free-fall. "I need you to come. Please come."

"I'm right there," I reply, breath hitching, catching in my throat. His swollen head brushes against mine as I grind against him, and with one more pump of his fingers against my prostate, I spray him down with my cum. "Oh, f-fuck, Eli. You're gonna kill me, aren't you?" I moan as my cock pulses, and his begins to throb and pulse too. His entire body tenses as he comes, and his fingers are still inside of me as he throws his head back and exposes his throat to me. I bite down on his Adam's apple, and he rocks his hips frantically, riding out his orgasm. "Oh, fuck me, you're so goddamn pretty."

Elijah's eyes fly open, lips parted as he pants, chest heaving rapid breaths. "Language," he scolds. "You curse too much."

I chuckle, shaking my head, but don't say anything. His eyes narrow on me momentarily, and then he's pulling his fingers out of me. It draws a hiss from my lips, and I feel a dull sting as he raises an eyebrow at me, clearly daring me to curse once more.

I don't do it.

Instead, I grin and get off him. There's cum everywhere. All over his chest and abs, his groin, dripping down his sides. It clings to his skin, and I get a rag and wet it with warm water, bringing it back to him to clean him up. His eyes immediately fly to my face when I do it, wiping gently and then folding it over, running it over my skin too. Blue orbs dip down to watch me as I run the rag over my groin, then my cock. He focuses on my cock, his eyes widening, his teeth clamping down on his bottom lip. He looks ready to go again, but I smirk and turn, putting the rag in his hamper.

I go back to him, nudging him with my hand until he scoots over, then get in bed with him and pull his back to my front. My arm is wrapped around his middle, my nose buried in the back of his head, soft hair tickling my nose.

"W-what in the world are you doing?" Elijah hisses, trying to disentangle himself from me, but I don't let him. Instead, I hold him tighter, sealing us together until not even an inch of space exists between us.

"Staying," I reply simply.

"You can't." He shakes his head, trying to sit up, but I hold him down again. "You'll be seen, Az."

"I won't," I assure him.

He hesitates momentarily, then relaxes into my hold, melting against my body. He feels hard and soft at the same time, and I can't even explain what this is doing to my head. I'm totally fucked. It feels like history is repeating itself, but worse. Because this time, I have no excuse. I've already been cast out, so who even cares if I keep him? But then that would mean handing over my heart again, and last time I did that, it was shattered.

What if they take him away from me again?

What if his faith is stronger than what we could ever have?

Fuck.

I really need to get out of my head.

Thick silence envelops us, and I can make out Elijah's shallow breaths like he's pressed up against my ear. He calms down after a few minutes, his chest rising and falling slower, and I smile against the back of his head.

"Tell me about you," I whisper, not wanting to be heard outside of the room. I have no idea how loud I was, and that can be dangerous here. It is the middle of the night though, so hopefully everyone is asleep.

"What do you want to know?" he asks, and his voice is hesitant.

"Everything," I reply, tightening my arm around his waist, and he tenses. "Anything."

"Uh." Elijah clears his throat. "I don't really know what to say if I'm being honest."

"Tell me about your childhood."

My prompt gives him pause, and I hear him suck in a sharp breath. He's stiff as a board in my arms, and I realize I've struck a nerve. But right as I'm about to tell him to forget about it, he speaks.

"My dad is a preacher," he tells me, relaxing into my hold once more. "He's always wanted me to become a man of God. Said I had no choice."

"There's always a choice," I tell him.

"I was doing good, too—before you came along and ruined it all for me."

"Are you sure I ruined it, Elijah?" I ask him slowly. "Or are you just looking for someone to blame?" Elijah makes a strangled sound at the back of his throat, and I hear him sniffle. *Oh, fuck.* "Eli? Flip over."

"No."

"Do it," I growl, tugging on him until he's turning to face me. "Show me that pretty face, Beloved."

"Don't call me that." He hiccups, covering his mouth as a sob escapes him.

I watch, equal parts transfixed and horrified as tears track down his cheeks. "Please don't cry, Elijah," I whisper, then lean in and kiss his tears away slowly, my lips trailing over slick skin. "I can't stand it."

"You have to leave me alone, Azriel," he says through trembling lips, and I shake my head quickly, because no way in hell am I doing that. "Please. I need to repent. I need—"

"You need me."

"Why do you even want me?" he spits, face turning angry. "I'm tainted. Dirty. Defiled."

I frown. "You're none of those things."

"Yes, I am," he says through gritted teeth. "There's something seriously wrong with me, and I need to purge it out of me."

"There's nothing wrong with you, Elijah," I growl, getting frustrated. My hand buries itself into his hair, and I yank his head back, forcing his tear-filled, deep blue eyes to connect with my own. "You're perfect just the way you are. In every way. There's not one thing about you I'd change. So fuck what anyone else thinks or says."

"Easy for you to say," he whispers, lips trembling, eyes closing, and more tears spilling over wet cheeks.

It physically pains me to see him this way, and I feel something ugly festering inside of me. Anger—at *him*. At everyone who's ever had anything negative to say about him.

"Listen to me, Elijah," I say with conviction. "These people have brainwashed you. You really think what's in the bible is real? God didn't write that —men did. Men who wanted us all to follow their rules without question. They want sheep, and you're not a sheep. You *can't* be."

"Why not?" he asks softly, eyes finally focused back on mine.

"I won't let you," I say through gritted teeth, hand sliding to the back of his head and bringing him closer to me until my forehead is pressed against his, and our lips brush. "You're mine now, and I won't let you be lied to anymore."

Elijah's lips quiver against mine ever so slightly. "I'm yours?"

"Mine," I whisper, kissing his bottom lip when his lips part at my admission. "And you're never escaping me. So stop trying."

"Promise me," he demands. "Swear you won't leave me. Even when it's hard."

"I won't leave you," I tell him. "Even when it's hard—I swear it."

Elijah crashes his lips to mine, whimpering when I thrust my tongue into his mouth, and I seal our bodies together once more. It's when he melts into me that I realize the magnitude of the situation. He's been shamed and cast out his entire life, and it's going to take another lifetime to fix all the damage they've done. I need to get him out of here. Now.

I just don't know if he'll ever be open to it.

Chapter 6
Elijah

I'm shaking head to toe in this confession booth. I should've never asked Father Jacob to give me a few minutes of his time, because now I've realized I don't really want to talk. If I tell him, if I admit to what I've done, I might as well pack my bags and leave. I won't be welcome here anymore, and that would mean losing everything. A lifetime of community, of belonging, but also a lifetime of shame. I shake my head, trying to dispel those thoughts from my brain, but it's useless.

Father Jacob is silent on the other side of the booth, and the mesh separating us doesn't make me feel more at ease if I'm being honest with myself. Instead, it has me trembling and filling me with doubt. Why would I do this to myself? To Azriel? He doesn't deserve this, right? He swore to me that he'd never desert me, yet here I am doing it to him.

No.

I can't do it.

Clearing my throat, I shake my head and wipe my sweaty hands on my jeans. "I made a mistake—"

"Tell me about your mistake," Father Jacob says calmly, though I know he's just pretending. I'm nothing to him. Just another mouth to feed in this seminary. "I'm here to listen, Elijah."

"That's the thing…" I whisper, raising my chin. "I don't really have anything to talk about. I thought I did, but I don't."

"How could you think that and then change your mind?" He tuts. "What sin did you commit?"

"I didn't—"

"You know only I can absolve you," he continues, ignoring me, "but I need to know what you did for the proper course of action."

"Like w-w-what?" I stammer.

"Penance. Prayers," he replies, sighing. "I must know, Elijah. Confess."

"I—" I shake my head again. "I had an unwelcome dream," I lie.

Father Jacob hums, seemingly pleased with my answer. "And what happened in this dream?"

"I laid with a woman." My voice trembles, and he clears his throat. "I didn't mean to. It happened on its own."

"I know," he replies, "You can't control what happens with your mind as you sleep."

"So I don't need to repent?" I ask with confusion.

"Oh, you do." Father Jacob sighs long and loud. "I

fear it's worse than I thought. If you're dreaming this, you must want it fiercely. It's in your subconscious. Tell me, Elijah, have you been thinking of this a lot?"

"No." I shake my head quickly, but even I hear the panic in my voice, the lie. "Absolutely not."

"You can tell me," he replies slowly. "If something deeper, something *unholy*, is going on...you can confess."

"There's not," I reiterate.

I almost swear it, but then I realize that would make the lie even worse. I'd surely go to hell at that point. Not that I don't think I won't. I'm absolutely damned after everything I've done with Azriel.

"Very well." Father Jacob sighs, and I can't tell if he believes me or not. "Two days of fasting should fix you right up and Praying the Rosary five times per day for the next week."

I gulp. "Yes, Father."

Father Jacob begins to pray over me softly, and tears sting my eyes, then suddenly trail down my cheeks. How did I get here? This can't be my life. This isn't me. I'm not the one punished for sinning. I would never admit to something like that. No, I'd punish myself in silence. So when did it become too much for me to bear alone?

"May almighty God have mercy on you and forgive your sins, then lead you to eternal life," Father Jacob says when he finishes his prayer. "Go in peace."

"Thanks be to God," I whisper, then all but run out of the confession booth.

I spend the next few hours in the library, studying the bible in silence and filling my journal with prayers about purity and doing the right thing. I skipped dinner as ordered by Father Jacob, and though my stomach is growling, I ignore the pain. I've done it before and will undoubtedly do it many more times. I swear, I always feel guilty about something.

Grabbing my bible and journal, I make my way past the rows of shelves and stop in my tracks when I see Gemma. She's staring at me intently as well and raises an eyebrow. Before I can run away, she blocks my path and crosses her arms over her chest. I swallow hard, trying to calm the erratic beating of my heart, but I think it's impossible. I feel lightheaded.

"I know what you've done," she whispers, and I stiffen. "I know you're a sinner just like me."

I shake my head. "I don't know what you're talking about."

"Azriel visits you, doesn't he?" Gemma asks, looking around to make sure no one is listening, but there's no one else here anyway. Just us. "You can tell me."

"I don't know who that is." I raise my shoulders nonchalantly. "Excuse me."

I try to walk past her, looking forward and

attempting to ignore her, but she blocks me yet again. I huff in annoyance, then remind myself I'm a man of God and we don't act like this.

"I know." She grins. "You don't have to admit it—I see it on your face. You're glowing, Elijah. I know you've been touched by sin."

Oh, God.

Please make her stop.

"Please excuse me, Gemma," I say with a shaking voice. "I have to go."

"As you wish," she mutters, stepping out of the way. "We could've bonded, you know."

I clear my throat and nod. "Maybe another time."

She lets me go, thankfully, and I all but sprint to the living quarters. I'm tired of interacting with people for the day, and yet, as soon as I make it to the living room, Micah is beckoning me to him. I give him a barely there smile, a very fake one, and his brows furrow.

My room feels so inviting right now, and I want to give him an excuse, *any* excuse, to finally be left alone. I just want to be one with my thoughts for a while. But I don't do that. Instead, I make my way to his side and sit on the couch with him. Resting my bible and journal on my lap, I face forward and stare at the wall across from us, right above the opposite couch.

He clears his throat. "Are you alright?"

"Yeah," I say hoarsely, then shake my head. "I don't know."

"You can talk to me."

"There's not much to say, Micah." I sigh. "Maybe I just need a distraction."

Micah smiles. "I can give you that."

I nod, smiling back. "Have you talked to your family?"

Micah wasn't raised in the church. He doesn't have a family that demanded perfection from him growing up. Maybe that's why he's more relaxed when it comes to this place. He follows God because he chooses to, not because he is expected to. There has to be a certain freedom in that, a weight lifted off his shoulders. The fear of failure is taken away because no one is pressuring him to go through with this. But then that makes me wonder, if he's doing it of his own free will, why in the world would he want to?

"Yeah," he says softly, and I look at him. He's smiling, his eyes shining with happiness. "Lucy just had her baby." His sister. "She named him Luca."

"I love that name," I whisper.

"Yeah, me too," he replies, smile faltering at my expression. I don't know what I look like right now, but I force myself to go blank. "She said they'll come to visit soon. They're only an hour away."

"That's nice." I smile, kind of wishing I had someone to visit me. But I'd never want my parents to come here. They'd just find a way to put me down in front of all the people I admire. No, that won't do. I've suffered enough humiliation from them. "I'm really glad, Micah."

"You can meet them…" he says softly. "I'd like you to."

"Sure, I'd love that," I reply, smile wobbling.

"Elijah, have you ever thought about leaving this place?" Micah asks me, and I frown. The seminary feels like home though, so I shake my head. "I have, you know. I don't really know if I have what it takes to go through with this."

"What do you mean?" I ask him, looking away. I know exactly what he means and why he's asking me. But I pretend I don't. I'm not sure why I want him to say it out loud, but I do.

"I think you know exactly what I mean," he whispers, getting closer to my ear. I look forward, feeling his warm breath on the shell of my ear. "Don't pretend you don't feel this too."

I gasp, staying still, not daring to move. "What are you saying, Micah?"

"I'm saying I—I like you." His voice trembles slightly, and my eyes widen when his fingers wrap around my forearm. "I want to be with you."

"Micah—"

"Let's leave," he says with more urgency, clearly sensing a rejection. "Let's go far away and live our lives together."

Oh, Jesus.

What have I done? Have I led him on? I'm not even sure anymore, but maybe I shouldn't have encouraged him to speak up.

I shake my head. "I c-can't," I whisper. "I've been raised for this my whole life, Micah. You wouldn't understand."

"No, I wouldn't," he replies, "I think we could be really happy. I'd make sure of it."

"I'm sorry, Micah." I sigh, extracting his fingers from my arm one by one. "I feel very tired, but I'll see you in the morning."

I make yet another mistake when I look at him—and what stares back at me makes my chest tighten. His eyes are bloodshot, and there are tears in them, but he looks away from me as they spill over. I almost reach out to wipe them off but decide against it. I don't want to make this worse.

"Sure."

I nod slowly, then get up and walk away.

Pushing open my bedroom door, I close it behind me and set my belongings on the desk. I begin to pace, burying my hands in my hair and yanking at the strands until my scalp stings. I feel like I need the pain to ground me, and even the one in my stomach isn't enough anymore. My exhale is shaky as I grab my rosary from the desk and set it on the bed. I take off my jeans but keep my underwear and shirt on, then kneel on the mattress. I face the wall above my headboard, reciting prayers and closing my eyes, and eventually, I press my forehead to the pillow and stay on my knees. With my rosary gripped in my fist, I let the tears run down my cheeks.

I'm not sure how long I stay this way, but I hear my lock click and snap out of my daze. I squeeze my eyes tighter, not daring to look, even though I know exactly who just walked in. My fist tightens, the beads of the rosary digging into my palm painfully, and I wince. It just reminds me of the reason I'm praying. For being a liar. I suppose I could always ignore the instructions Father Jacob gave me, but then who would I be if I did that? I've already messed up beyond belief.

"Is my pretty little liar begging for forgiveness?" Azriel's voice breaks through my thoughts, making me clench my pillow between my fingers.

I whimper, not daring to move as my tears soak the pillow. I can barely breathe through my nose from how much I've been crying, but I won't be moving from this position. I refuse to.

"Elijah, I'm talking to you." He warns, "I don't like being ignored."

"Go away, Azriel," I tell him, voice muffled by my pillow. I shift my face to the side so he can hear me better, when I see that he's climbing into bed and kneeling behind me. I stiffen. "Please."

He doesn't reply. Instead, he grabs me by my hair and yanks me up until I'm on my knees, his front flush with my back. His cock is nestled between my ass cheeks, hard as a steel rod. My nostrils flare when his free hand wraps around my throat, and I begin to shake when his lips press against the shell of my ear.

"You want to know what I think?" he asks softly, and I shake my head. I don't want to know. I want him to leave me be. I need a night to myself. I think he's done enough damage for a lifetime. "I think if these tears are for your God, I'm going to be really pissed off."

Azriel's fingers tighten around my throat until I can't take in a breath, then release slightly. His fingers are still clutching the strands of my hair painfully, and I exhale a shaky breath as he grinds his cock against me.

"Go away," I demand, but my voice trembles, and if I'm being honest with myself, I don't really want him to. I want him to fight for me, but I'd never admit to it. Because at the same time, I feel like I need to fight for myself. For what's best for me. I need to fight for my faith. "I demand it."

"You demand it?" Azriel chuckles, and a shiver runs down my spine. "Let me make something clear to you, Elijah." His grip tightens on my hair until more tears spill from my eyes, and the hand around my throat shifts to the middle of my back. He shoves me down once more, pushing my face into the pillow. I'm on my knees now, back arched, ass in perfect alignment with his cock. Open for him. Pliant but not. "You only kneel for *me*."

"That's absurd, and you know it," I say, trying to buck him off.

"Stop fighting me," he growls. "It just makes me want to turn you inside out even more."

"You're not doing anything to me," I grit out.

"No?" Azriel tuts, letting go of me abruptly. I immediately miss the heat of his body against me and almost whimper at the loss of him. That is, until his fingers dig into my hips, tugging my underwear over my ass and down my thighs. "I think you'd do just about anything to have me in that tight little ass."

"Don't say that."

"Why, Little Lamb?" he mocks. "Afraid your God will find out? I bet he already knows."

"Shut up," I growl, and I don't think I've ever been this angry in my life. "Shut. Up."

A sudden sting has me bucking forward, away from him. He just *spanked* me. I groan, my balls tightening and my cock filling quickly with blood. Just when I think he's done, two more swats land on my ass in rapid succession. I whimper, shaking my head, about to protest when I feel his breath against my hole. I clench, scared yet exhilarated all the same. I want him there, and he knows it. He knows how to play me like an instrument.

I've never stood a chance against him.

"This pretty ass belongs to me," he whispers,

kissing my cheek slowly, dragging his tongue over my skin until he's close to my crease. "*You* belong to me."

"Azriel."

"Beg me, Eli," Az chokes out, his voice hoarse. "Beg me to fill your ass. Beg me to ruin you."

"You've already ruined me," I whisper.

"You're going to worship me," he says through gritted teeth, and I can hear the anger in his voice as he tilts my hips further up. "You're going to beg for anything I want to give you, and you're going to do it from your fucking knees, Elijah, or lying to your priest will be the least of your worries."

I tremble. "You know?"

"I know everything," he replies harshly. "I see everything."

The cap of a bottle opening sounds like an explosion in the silence of the room, but I refuse to look. A cold container rolls toward my thigh, and this time I open my eyes and see that it's lube. I frown, but then there are cold fingers pressing to my entrance, and my eyes widen.

"I don't know if I want this, Azriel," I say quickly. "Wait—"

"Give me a good reason," he says calmly, and my mind goes blank. "I don't think you have one."

"I—" I choke when Azriel's fingers drag down my crease, spreading the lube over my hole. It's cold and sticky, and I shudder when the pad of one of his fingers rubs a circle over my rim. "*Az.*"

"Yes, Beloved?" he asks softly, and when I look over my shoulder, his eyes are intense, and his lips are set in a smirk. My eyes widen when he pushes the tip of his finger into me, and the burn takes my breath away. "Relax for me. Let me in this pretty little hole."

I take a deep breath, forcing my body to relax, and moan when more of his finger pushes into me. I remember the way I fingered him, rough and demanding, punishing, and almost flinch. He's taking it easy on me, when instead, he let me have revenge on him. I don't think I deserve this much softness, but I stay quiet.

"Y-yes," I whisper, pushing my ass back a little, his finger slipping all the way in. He withdraws it, then pushes two inside of me simultaneously. I moan, feeling the sting all the way down to my toes, but when he begins to thrust his fingers in and out of me, my toes curl for a different reason. One that isn't pain. Because right now, as he curls his fingers just like I did to him, all I feel is pleasure. "Oh, yes, *baby*, please."

Azriel growls deep in his chest, pumping his fingers harder. "Baby, huh?"

His fingers rub over a sensitive spot inside of me, one that lights me up from the inside out, and my eyes roll to the back of my head. I bite my bottom lip to keep my sounds in, and Azriel goes even harder and faster. I think he's doing it on purpose. He wants to hear me, but I refuse.

"No." I shake my head. "I didn't mean to say that."

"You want this," he says softly, and I can hear the smirk in his voice even though I'm not watching him. It's odd that I can see it in my head with my eyes closed, but I can. "Admit it."

"If I want this, I must be wicked," I whisper.

"Then why does it feel like grace, Little Lamb?" His voice is sensual and low, doing strange things to my stomach.

The way his fingers work me deep inside feels unlike anything I've ever felt before, and I reach between my legs and start tugging on my cock quickly, chasing relief. I practically sob at the pleasure quickly building up, at the way my spine begins to tingle. My balls feel like they're about to explode, and just as I'm about to finish, Azriel pulls his fingers out and leaves me empty.

I make a whimpering sound in protest.

"I can do this all night, Elijah," Azriel says softly, running a hand down my spine, fingers digging into my ass cheek and parting me. My face heats. Does he like what he sees? "Give me what I want."

I frown, confused. "W-what do you want?"

"All of you."

I shake my head. "Not that."

"You'll give me what I want." Azriel smirks. "It's just a matter of time."

Turning my head, I look at him. His eyes are glued to my ass, which I realize, is still on full display for him. I'm spread open, knees apart, back arched. My balls are full, my cock throbbing between my legs to the beat of my heart. I'd do just about anything to come at this point.

"Just—" I clear my throat. "*Please.*"

"What are you asking for?" He smirks, raising an eyebrow as his eyes connect with mine. "Hmm?"

"God, *please*, just let me come," I whimper, touching myself, wrapping a hand around my cock once more, and jerking it slowly. My toes curl at the pleasure, and Azriel's hand lands on my ass for a hard slap. "I need to come."

"I'm not God," he growls. "If you're going to beg me, at least say my fucking name."

"*Azriel.*"

"Yes, Little Lamb?"

"Please," I choke out. "I'll do anything—"

"Get on your back." He cuts me off. "Legs spread."

I flip over onto my back so quickly my head spins, and then, as if I haven't already humiliated myself enough, I spread my legs wide and hold my thighs open for him. He looks at me with hungry eyes, his gaze focused on my cock, which is bright red and engorged. I feel like I'm going to go out of my mind if he doesn't do something soon, and as if he can hear my thoughts, he grabs the lube once more and gathers some on his fingers.

"Such a good boy when you want something from me, aren't you?" He grins, and his eyes light up in a way I've never seen from him before. It makes my heart skip several beats, and I gulp at the feeling. It's one thing to want him for this, and it's something else entirely to want him for more. I can't do that. I won't. "Touch yourself, Elijah."

I sigh in relief and wrap a hand around my cock, jerking slowly as I watch him. My lids are hooded, heavy, and I'm fighting to keep my eyes open. He shakes his head, smirking.

"That's not what I meant." He tuts, "I want you to suck on your fingers and stuff them in your ass."

I shiver, bringing my fingers to my lips and sucking on them. He nods slowly, and I drag my hand down my torso, watching as he stares in fascination. I reach my entrance, and then, hesitantly, I push past the ring of muscle trying to keep me out. I'm already open, my hole willing, and it doesn't take much resistance to stuff myself full. Pumping my fingers in and out, my cock jerks when I rub over my prostate, and my back bows off the bed.

I'm panting now, breathing hard. "I need you," I moan, my voice raspy, and Azriel swallows hard, cock standing at full mast. "Please, Azriel, come here."

Azriel crawls toward me and settles between my legs, holding them up while I pump my fingers in and out of my hole, and I let out a garbled sound that I don't even recognize when he wraps his hand around my cock and jerks it for me.

"You prayed to be filled," Azriel whispers sinfully, pressing a finger to my entrance right next to my other two. He pushes in, directing my digits toward my prostate, and the feeling of fullness in my ass is propelling me toward my orgasm. "Shall I answer?"

"P-please," I groan. "I'm begging you. *Please*. I need your cock."

"Not yet, Little Lamb," Azriel says, and my eyes fill with tears. "You will ask properly."

"Give me your cock, Azriel," I growl, startling myself, and he chuckles. He withdraws his finger from inside of me, and I get up on my knees, grabbing his shoulders and pushing him down onto the bed until his back hits the mattress. I straddle him, gripping his chest with my fingers and squeezing. He's thick, muscular, and doesn't even flinch. I know I'm being rough, but he doesn't seem phased in the slightest. "I want it."

"You want it that bad, Elijah?" he asks. "So turn around and suck it. Let me have that pretty ass while you choke on me."

I whimper, and despite not feeling confident, I do as I'm told. His cock is huge and thick as I grab it in my fist and hold it up to my mouth. A bead of precum sits at the slit, and I lick it gingerly. Azriel's hips buck, and he thrusts into my fist.

"Do you need a demonstration?" His voice is soft but hoarse. "I'll go first."

Azriel grabs my cock, and the next thing I know, it's in his mouth. The velvety softness of his lips engulfs me, the warmth and wetness of his tongue as it twirls around my tip making me cry out. He grabs my hips and controls the pace, not sucking, instead he's making me thrust into his mouth. I can feel the back of his throat contracting as he chokes, and when he lets go of my hips, I slow down my thrusts. His fingers prod at my entrance once more, and when he fills me, curling his digits deep inside of me, I almost scream. I have to swallow his cock down to shut up, yet I'm still a whimpering mess even with a cock all the way in the back of my throat.

I choke and gag, pulling back, but every time I do, he hits my prostate with his fingers, and I go down on him all the way to keep myself from screaming. I'm close already, practically humping his face as I get closer to my climax, and he begins to moan with my cock in his mouth.

Saliva drips down the sides of my mouth and down his balls as I suck him down and choke on him, and I use it to coat my fingers and move them down to his hole. I rub it in slow circles, but just before I breach him, he begins to shake and starts to come in my mouth. The sounds he's letting out vibrate my balls, and I groan loudly as I feel my orgasm tackle me and hold me under. He's still coming and coming and coming. And I am too. We can't stop. Why is it dragging on and on?

It feels *so* damn good.

Azriel withdraws his fingers slowly, giving me time to adjust, and I let him slip from between my lips. My throat feels raw, and I grimace as I swallow once more, tasting his cum. But instead of getting up, I pull out of his mouth and lie my head on his thigh, putting my weight on him once more.

And I just…close my eyes.

After a while, I forget about everything. He doesn't move, and when my world goes black, he lets me sleep on him. It's only a few hours later—when it's still dark—that I realize that he's gone. And then it hits me…

I don't want to be without him anymore.

Chapter 7
azriel

The chapel is empty as I pace back and forth in the shadows, considering going to Elijah's room again, but realizing I need to calm down before I do. I'm angry. Well, that is an understatement. Rage is simmering in my blood, and if I see him, I know I'm going to demand answers. Watching him and his friend be all over each other in the chapel this morning is making me come undone. I hate that Micah had his hands all over him.

I stop and stare at the spot where he had been sitting with his friend Micah just hours ago, speaking in hushed whispers. I saw the way they looked at each other, and fuck, something possessive threatened to take over and yank Elijah away from the man. But I didn't. Somehow, I stayed hidden, always in the shadows, forever separated from his life until nighttime when he gives himself over to me. The only time he lets me—in the dark, where no one will know.

He's willing to be seen in the light with Micah though, which makes something ugly crawl inside my chest. The way he touched Elijah's wrist and said his name as if it meant something holy haunts me. Just remembering it is making me shake with rage. I was jealous, I *am* jealous.

Mine.

Elijah is fucking *mine.*

Speak of the devil, and he shall appear—Elijah is walking toward the chapel. He hesitates at the threshold before walking toward the altar, the candles burning low, lighting his path. He's as quiet as a mouse, clearly not wanting to be discovered, and my nostrils flare when his steps hurry even more. He stops in front of the altar and grabs an unlit candle, placing it in front of him and grabbing matches to light it. Once the flame is lit, he takes a step back and bows his head.

Elijah exhales shakily, loudly, as if bothered by something. Maybe he's remembering something himself—something worth praying about. Something making him beg for forgiveness. Maybe it's about me, or maybe it's about Micah. Either way, it pisses me off even more.

Anger propels me forward, and I make sure to tuck my wings in, since I'm no longer in my human form, as I walk down the aisle from behind him and stop a few feet away. He doesn't notice me, his head still bowed, whispers coming from his lips. I can't make out what he's saying, but it sounds like he's begging his God for something. Absolution, probably. Doesn't he know he won't get it? His God isn't kind or understanding, and yet he's worshipped anyway.

"He touched you, Elijah," I say softly and watch as his body stiffens and he gasps.

Elijah startles, turning around. He looks terrified, yet instantly aroused at seeing me. He also seems intrigued, and more than a little confused. His wide eyes roam my naked body, and then come back up to my face, blue orbs boring into my golden ones. I look down to notice his erection tenting his jeans. My Little Lamb, always horny for me.

"You were watching me?" he murmurs, barely audible, and I narrow my eyes at him.

"I'm always watching you, Elijah."

"He's just a friend," he says, lips wobbly.

I take a step forward, then another, until I'm crowding him. "Is that what you call it when your breath hitches and your pulse stammers beneath someone else's hands?"

Elijah shakes his head, taking a step back, but stopping before he can burn himself with his candle. The fucking candle he lit to pray to his God. To beg for forgiveness. "Az, that's not fair—"

I almost give up the fight altogether when my

name falls from his lips. When he's shortened it. Made it his own. But I don't.

"Fair?" I spit, caging him against the altar, moving the candle to the corner so I can rest my hands on either side of him. He trembles beautifully, panting breaths falling from his lips. Lips I want to fucking devour but refuse to. "You summoned me. Named me. You offered me your desire, and I came. And now you dare to tremble for another man?"

"Micah didn't mean anything by it."

"Maybe not." I narrow my eyes on him. "But you did."

Elijah stays quiet as I press my body to his, anger boiling and spilling over. My chest rises and falls against his, and the warmth of him is enough to make me spiral. I feel like a feral animal trying not to show my teeth, and I'm definitely failing.

"Did he touch you here?" I ask against the shell of his ear, brushing his wrist with my fingers lightly. "Did he whisper your name as if it's sacred? Did he see how you bend so prettily when you're close to breaking?"

Elijah gasps, and my nostrils flare as I try to rein myself in. But it's impossible. I feel sharp. Possessive. All consuming.

"Why does it matter?"

I pull back and lean into his face instead, our foreheads almost touching, and now we're sharing breath. "Because you're mine," I whisper. "Because when you cry out in the dark, I answer. Not him. *Me.*"

Elijah sucks in a sharp breath, his bottom lip trembling, his eyes filling with tears. It reminds me of a few nights ago when I visited him and he had this same expression on his face. When guilt was eating him alive. I left him alone after that, trying to convince myself that it wasn't meant to be. That he'd never accept me into his life. He's too busy trying to serve his God, his church, his brothers. There's no space for me there, and I convinced myself to let him be. Until today, when I realized I couldn't see him with another man. One who clearly wants him. I let it go the other night because Elijah rejected him, but he's clearly not giving up.

I'm not letting Elijah go.

Not now.

Not ever.

"If he touches you again, I'll tear him from your memory," I growl against his lips, tilting my face until our noses brush, and I feel his lips shiver against mine.

Elijah flinches. "You'd hurt him? My best friend?"

"If you want me to," I whisper, brushing my knuckles against his cheek and fighting the urge to press my lips to his. "Do you?"

Elijah doesn't speak, but his body says everything I need to know. My hand slips around his throat, not tight, just claiming. Elijah shivers, making a needy little sound at the back of his throat.

"Say it," I growl. "Tell me who you belong to."

Elijah closes his eyes, and I feel his pulse pounding against the palm of my hand. My chest heaves as I wait for his words, and even though it's just a split second, it feels like an eternity.

"You."

I smile. "Show me."

Elijah gasps, then crashes his lips to mine. He kisses me like he's sealing a covenant, lips parting until he sucks on my bottom lip roughly. He's lost to passion, biting and tugging at my lip, completely out of control. He thrusts his tongue into my mouth impatiently, and I suck on it until a groan tears from his throat.

Elijah pulls away, eyes wide.

"Strip," I command, taking a few steps back and giving him space.

He immediately obeys, taking off his clothes and letting them drop to the ground by his feet. His bare back is now to the altar, his tan body on full display, cock hanging heavily between his legs, thickening before my eyes. I look up to find him biting his bottom lip, eyes boring into mine with a fire I've never seen burning so brightly within him. He wants this. Me. Us.

I can tell.

"Do you give yourself to me?" I ask him with a

whisper, my ashen wings spreading behind me. His eyes widen as he takes me in. "Willingly?"

There's a pause from him, eyes wide as he considers my words. He bites his bottom lip as he thinks about it, a frown on his face, and just when I think he's going to reject me, he speaks again.

"Yes." Elijah nods slowly, cock fully hard, and he wraps his hand around it tightly until his knuckles blanch. "I burn for you, Azriel."

A shiver runs down my spine as I grab his ass and lift him onto the altar, laying him on his back and spreading his legs. I kiss a path down his chest, down his abs, then take his cock into my mouth. His head falls back as he moans and trembles for me, and I let him go, trailing my lips lower. I lift his balls and look at his hole, my eyes widening. He prepped for me. He's slightly open and glistening with the lube I left for him in his drawer.

I thrust two fingers into him, and he cries out, then thrust a third one in. He clenches around my fingers when I find that little spot of pleasure inside of him, and I watch as his cock turns a deep shade of red. He reaches for it, about to wrap his hand around it to chase relief, but I swat it away with my free hand and continue to finger him. He makes a choked noise at the back of his throat, and we make eye contact.

"You'll come on my cock or nowhere at all, Elijah," I growl, "I'm not playing any more games with you. I'm taking you right here, right now."

"Yes," he gasps when I push him back on the altar a few inches, and he spreads his legs wider. "I need you, give me your cock. Please. Right n-now."

"Such a demanding little creature." I tut, then climb onto the altar with him, getting between his legs and pressing them up toward his chest. "Tell me you're mine."

"I'm yours," Elijah moans when I bite his chest, drawing blood. "More."

I look beside me, at the candle burning brightly, and grab it. Elijah's eyes widen when I pour the wax onto his chest, and he hisses. I look down as his cock jerks against his abdomen, and I smirk. Looks like my little lamb likes a little bit of pain.

"So beautiful, Eli," I whisper reverently, "So beautiful and so fucking mine."

"*Yes.*"

Elijah holds his knees up to his chest as I press my cock against his hole, notching it at his entrance, but before I go through with it, I want to do one last thing. One last ritual.

I grab the anointing oil next to his head and open it, dripping some onto my fingers and pressing them to his forehead. I draw the sign of the cross, then say, "I consecrate this oil to claim you, Elijah. Body, mind, and soul. From this day forward, you belong to me, and I to you. You'll be everything to me from now until eternity. My love, my religion, my ruin."

Elijah shakes underneath me. "Forever?"

"Always," I assure him.

"Fill me, Azriel," he growls, eyes crazy, desperate. Just how I like him. "Fill me with holy fire. Take me apart and put me back together."

I don't wait one more second, drenching my cock in oil and gripping it tightly. I push into him slowly, and it feels like a vise around my cock when the head finally breaks through the ring of muscle. I clench my eyes shut and breathe in deeply through my nose, then push in another inch. Elijah whimpers, and my eyes fly open.

"It's okay," I say softly. "Relax for me, Eli."

"Oh, f-f-fuck," he mewls, eyes squeezing shut as I push in another inch, then another, and another, until I look down at his cock to watch it dripping between us. I wrap a hand around him, jacking him off as I push in further. "Yes. Please. All the way."

Elijah's fingers dig into my shoulders as I bottom out, and there's a moment between us that feels like a lifetime, yet I know it's just a split second. We look into each other's eyes, his searching mine frantically, and I nod at him. I'm reassuring him with that nod. That this is it for me, that he's it for me. I want nothing else except for him. We're tied together, bound, from now until eternity.

Infinity.

Stained glass glows red from the moonlight, and I look back down at him, raising an eyebrow.

"Ready?" I ask through gritted teeth, trying to keep my composure as his heat envelops me.

"Azriel," he moans. "Please move. I need you to move."

And just like that, I pull back and thrust back in.

It's heaven and hell.

It's my undoing.

I *want* him to destroy me.

I'm willing.

Chapter 8
Elijah

The burn of the stretch is all-encompassing. Azriel is filling my body to bursting, spreading me to my limit. I can feel him in my very atoms as he pulls back and thrusts back in, filling me so completely it feels like all of my cells have been rearranged. At the same time, I've never felt so whole, so completely in tune with someone else. Like a puzzle piece that was missing, fitting back into place. The very last one.

I gasp as Azriel spreads my legs as he leans into my body. I wrap my thighs around his waist as he nails my prostate over and over, my mouth opening up on a guttural moan that comes from the depths of my soul. His teeth clamp around my earlobe, and he bites down softly, making a shiver run down my spine, and my balls tighten. He knows what he's doing as he swipes his tongue down the slope of my neck and sucks on my pulse point, dragging his teeth over it.

Whimpers and whines are ripped from my throat

as he buries his face into the crook of my neck, his warm breath against my skin bringing me even closer to the edge. Azriel braces himself on one forearm next to my face as he uses his free hand to wrap around my cock, and his tight grip moving up and down at the same time as he hits that one spot inside of me over and over is my undoing.

I moan loudly, barely able to hear Azriel's throaty groans over the sounds of my pleasure. My balls tighten, and I plant my feet on the altar and begin to top from the bottom.

"Yes, Elijah," Azriel moans against my ear, and I mewl. "Fuck yourself on my cock. Spill all over my fist."

"*There*," I groan. "Don't stop. Please. Don't—don't—"

Sweet relief washes over me as I do exactly what he demanded, spilling over his fist, my body tensing as the most intense orgasm of my life takes hold of me and rattles my bones.

"Does my sweet boy like his slutty little hole filled?" Azriel whispers against the shell of my ear, and I clench around his cock. "My perfect little fuck hole."

My chest heaves as I come back into my body, feeling more than seeing as Azriel slows down and stops altogether. I frown, confusion snapping me out of the little bubble I've been in, because he hasn't come yet. He straightens, letting go of my cock and grabbing something from beside him. A silver knife.

"Swear to be mine," Azriel chokes out, and I nod quickly, eyes wide. "Prove it to me."

"H-how?" I stammer.

"Seal this bond between us," Azriel replies, and I watch in rapt fascination as he slices his palm and holds it over my face. Blood drips onto my skin, warm and sticky, and he looks at me expectantly. "Drink me."

I part my lips slightly, and Azriel presses his hand between them, forcing them to open more. I suck hard, drinking his blood, savoring the coppery-sweet taste before he rips it away from my mouth and smears it down my face.

"Mine," I groan. "You're mine, Azriel. I'll never let you go now."

Azriel grabs my hand and presses it to his chest, holding it there as he pushes forward once more and impales me on his length. I cry out, my body moving up on the altar with the force of his thrusts. My hand grips his chest, fingers digging in the faster and deeper he goes. It turns red from his blood, and I'm mesmerized. Absolutely hypnotized by the angel above me. Because that's what he is. My angel, my salvation, and also my sweet damnation.

"Hide me from God," I whimper as Azriel goes faster, and he lets go of my hand, leaning down and covering my body with his. "Please, baby, don't let him see my ruin."

Azriel's wings spread above us momentarily, and then he wraps me in them tightly. I'm in a cocoon of warmth as he fucks me deeper, like he's trying to embed himself inside of me.

"I'll keep you safe," Azriel vows. "Now." Thrust. "Forever." Thrust. "Always." Thrust.

"Yes," I moan, his abdomen rubbing against my cock with every thrust. It's lighting me up from the inside out, and before I even know what's going on, I'm close again. "I'm gonna—"

"Come for me again, Beloved," Azriel begs. "I want to fill you. Mark you. Claim you as mine."

"*Oh*. Mmmm," I moan. "I'm gonna come! I'm gonna come for you."

"That's it, my good boy," Az growls against my ear, going faster now, hitting my prostate over and over. "So good for me."

I'm tense as I feel my cock erupt, spurts of hot cum landing between us, all the way up to my throat. "Azriel!" The way he keeps rubbing against my sensitive length makes me shudder, and I gasp. "F-fuck."

"My name sounds divine coming from your lips, Little Lamb," he groans, lifting himself off me and getting on his knees between my legs. His hand wraps around my throat as he slams into me with a force so powerful I feel like he's going to come out of my mouth. "This ass was made to take me. So good, Elijah. So fucking tight."

"It's yours," I say. "All yours."

I watch, mesmerized, as Azriel's hips slap against my ass and he bites on his bottom lip. His abs are soaked with my cum, glistening in the low candlelight, and I grip his thighs with my fingers, needing to feel him. I haven't touched him much, and I'm starting to regret that.

He doesn't seem real as I stare up at him, broad shoulders, thick chest, trim waist leading down to a huge cock that's currently splitting me in half. His golden eyes stare into mine, dark curls unruly over his forehead, beautiful ashen wings spread once more. Absolutely stunning.

Azriel tenses, his moans crescendo, and hot liquid fills my insides. I moan in surprise at how warm it feels, and he pulls out and looks between my legs. He jumps off the altar, grabbing my thighs and dragging me until my ass is resting on the edge of it. Then he thrusts two fingers inside of me and presses them against my prostate, massaging me from the inside out. I groan, and he pulls away.

"Push it out, Beloved," Azriel says softly, still staring at my hole, and my cheeks heat. "Let me see what I filled you with."

"Oh, fuck." I groan as he pushes another finger in again, and I push out slightly, feeling hot liquid drip out of me. "It's so hot."

"You have no idea," he growls, then kneels between my thighs and pushes his tongue into me. I practically levitate off the altar, my eyes squeezing shut at the overwhelming pleasure.

"W-what are you doing?" I croak, suddenly embarrassed.

"Not letting any of this go to waste, Little Lamb," he says against my ass, lips pressed against my hole. He kisses it softly. "Not even one drop."

"*Oh.*"

I moan when his tongue thrusts inside of me once more, and he doesn't stop until he's satisfied, and my cock is hard again. And just when I think I can't take it anymore, when I'm so wound up I feel like I'll burst, he begs me to give him one more. Another one just for him. And I do. I come down his throat, fucking it as his fingers curl deep inside of me.

If hell exists, I know I'll be there.

Now more than ever.

But I'm starting to realize…I don't even care anymore.

Chapter 9
Elijah

Evening prayer is the same as always, and I swear I'm trying to pay attention, but with my bowed head, all I've managed to do is think about last night. The way Azriel filled me so perfectly, so wholly, that nothing else mattered in that moment. And it still doesn't. I feel complete, finally. Nevertheless, a very scared part of me wonders if this is real, and how it'll even work out. What happens if I leave this place behind? What will I do? What will *he* do? Is he even able to be by my side as a real partner, or will I forever see him in secret? In the dead of night, when no one will know he exists except for me?

Somehow, I know I'd continue to do that if it's what it takes to be with him. I'm that far gone. I'd rather have him in secret than not at all, and that seems a bit problematic. If I'm going to leave everything behind—the church, the community I've revolved around my entire life, and even my relationship with God—I need to know that he will be by my side forever. That he's truly all in. There has to be a way for him to live by my side as a partner. A real one. At least that should be my expectation, right? So why does it feel like I'd take whatever scraps he offered to me? That can't be how I act. It can't. I have to really think about this.

"*Amen*," Father Jacob says cheerfully, but I continue to bow my head, eyes squeezed shut, almost afraid to open them.

Micah nudges my shoulder with his, and I open my eyes and turn my head to look at him. His eyes are red-rimmed as if he's been crying, and I frown. He continues to stare at me, wide green eyes looking into mine, and I don't even notice when someone calls my name until they say it the second time. More urgently. With a bit of a kick to it.

"Brother Elijah," Father Jacob repeats for a third time. "Will you please come here?"

I stiffen because if he wants me to come to him, it's for a reason. He doesn't isolate any of us unless it's serious. Suddenly, my hands turn clammy, and I wipe them on my pants. He waits patiently for me to stand and turn my body toward him, and once I do, I give him a wide fake smile. But it's what I have to do —pretend. To be alright. The picture of sainthood. God, not only have I become a fornicator, but I've also turned into a liar of epic proportions.

"Yes, Father?" I ask softly once I reach him, stopping a few feet away.

MEANT TO BURN

The chapel is now empty save for Micah, who remains in the pew where we were seated together just moments ago. His eyes narrow on us, but he doesn't move, and for that I'm grateful. I'll use him as my escape plan. A sweet excuse to cut this conversation short.

Sister Ruth stands next to Father Jacob, and my heart begins to pound so loudly in my ears that I can barely hear when he speaks. That would be a mercy though, and I find myself cursing the day I learned to read lips. They're watching me intently, looking for some sort of indication I refuse to give them. Instead, I keep my smile firmly in place, and I will continue to do so, even if it kills me.

"I've been watching you closely, Elijah," Father Jacob says, staring into my eyes. I gulp, faintly aware of Micah staring at my back. Father Jacob's eyes look weird, and this is the first time I think he seems to be the evil one in this situation. I'm not even sure why that thought invades my mind, but I push it to the side so I can pay attention. "I noticed you've been acting strangely."

"Strange how?" I ask, feeling increasingly more nervous the more he speaks.

"You've been distracted, which is unusual for you." His eyes narrow on my face. "Is something wrong? Have you been led astray?"

I gasp, feigning horror. "Absolutely not." Biggest

lie of the century, but I must commit to the bit, or I'll lose the plot.

"If you have, you can speak freely." Father Jacob raises an eyebrow, and Sister Ruth clears her throat daintily. "If you repent, all will be well. But you must confess and beg for forgiveness, or we can't help you."

"Nothing is wrong," I whisper, cracking a bit. I'm not sure I'm strong enough for this interrogation. "I'm the same man you've known all this time."

Father Jacob narrows his eyes at me, and I swallow hard, looking down at my shoes. I notice the scuffs on one of them, unable to bring myself to look up at him once more. All the attention is making me feel small and meek, and I bet he does see the wicked little liar I've become. Well, huge liar at this point.

"Lying won't help you," Father Jacob snarls, looking me up and down. Has he always been this vicious? This…hostile? It's almost like he's a different person all of a sudden.

"I'm not lying," I say with more confidence, raising my chin.

"Are you sure?" Sister Ruth asks, clearly intervening. "I can sense something is off. I see your soul has been stained black, but it's not too late for you to come clean."

I shake my head, tears threatening to fall at this point. "No. I'm fine."

He nods solemnly, clearly unhappy that I haven't

confessed, and he can't kick me out. He's probably bored in this seminary. Well, he can pick on someone else. Not me.

Wow, where did that come from?

"You're dismissed," Father Jacob says roughly, and I nod.

I walk back to Micah, who is waiting for me with a frown on his face. I don't stop though, and he scrambles out of the pew to follow after me.

"What was that?" Micah asks, catching up to me. "Why do they think you're doing something wrong? You're a saint."

"I'm *not* a saint," I mutter. "I don't know, alright? This isn't the first time they've questioned me." But I don't go into any more detail, and my friend is clearly not satisfied.

"You've been acting strange lately, you know. I guess I can see why they'd be worried," he murmurs, and I stiffen. Not him too. Anyone but Micah. He knows me well enough to know when I'm lying. "You can trust me. I won't say anything if you tell me what's going on."

"Nothing is going on." I sigh. "And honestly, I'm getting really tired of people implying there is. I'm perfectly fine, same as always. I'm just tired is all."

"All the time?" Micah asks, raising an eyebrow at me. My cheeks heat as I recall why I really am tired all the time. All of my midnight escapades. "Have you not been getting sleep?"

"Uh." I shake my head. "Not really."

"Hmmm," Micah murmurs, and I don't look at him, avoiding eye contact at all costs so he doesn't catch me in yet another lie. "If you need someone to hang out with when you're unable to sleep, I'm here."

"Thanks." I smile, this time looking at him. His own smile is wide, and his cheeks heat in a way that makes me believe he wouldn't only want to talk during this hangout session. Or maybe my brain is just depraved now that I've had a taste of true sin. Yeah, that's probably it.

I'd been walking blindly this entire time. For a moment, back at the chapel, I was leading the way, but now it's definitely Micah. Before I realize it, we've ended up in front of my bedroom door. I'm standing with my back against it, and Micah is crowding me. Everyone seems to be at dinner right now, which doesn't bode well for me, mostly because Micah is clearly feeling bolder than usual. He steps into me until our shoes are touching and leans into my face. He's a few inches away, and I can feel his breath against my lips.

Past me would've been elated at this turn of events but present me is actually terrified. I haven't forgotten how Azriel reacted to Micah, and I won't be the reason we have issues again. *No.* Micah is no one in comparison to my Azriel, and I have to put a stop to this. Right now.

"Micah—" I whisper, shaking my head quickly

when he leans into me, but he grabs my face with both hands. "Wait."

"I've waited long enough," he replies hoarsely, crushing his lips to mine.

They're hard and unyielding, and I turn my hand on the knob and open the door, letting my body push it open. I fall to the ground on my ass, and Micah manages not to topple over with me, thankfully. I don't know what I'd do if he ended up on top of me, but I'd probably knee him in the balls if it meant proving to Azriel that he's the only one for me.

"What the fuck, Elijah?" he spits, eyes narrowed on me, and I flinch. He's never spoken to me in that tone—*never*. "Is it really that unbearable to kiss me?"

"Micah—I'm sorry," I reply, breathing raggedly. Seriously, it sounds like I just ran a mile. "I told you to wait. I told you the other day that I don't want to be together. I'm sorry, but I don't want to lead you on."

"I see the way you look at me..." Micah trails off. "Why are you lying?"

"I'm *not* lying," I tell him desperately, wishing he'd believe me. I get up from the ground and wipe my sweaty hands on my hips. "If I wanted you, I'd be the first one to tell you to leave together. I'd be right there with you. But I don't reciprocate your feelings. I am sorry."

"Fuck this," Micah spits, turning around and leaving me behind.

He doesn't go very far, only walking a few feet to the left and opening his bedroom door, then slamming it shut. I exhale loudly in relief, shutting my own door and locking it for good measure. I sit down at my desk to write in my journal, which I've been doing every day since I met Azriel for the first time. Well, summoned him. Same thing. I've had to be careful with what I write, not wanting to implicate myself if someone finds it. So I've been writing in riddles, which is proving to be both difficult and fun. This time, when I open my journal to a new page, there's a note scribbled onto the paper.

Meet me in the confessional booth at eleven-thirty tonight.

- A

A flutter runs through me and lands in my stomach, making me feel queasy. The smile that takes over my face can only be described as radiant, and it's so wide it hurts my cheeks. I'm honestly grateful he can't see me making a fool of myself right now. I can't help it though. There's something about him that has done me in. I've fallen badly, and I know there's no possible way to hide it anymore.

I spend the next few hours writing in my journal and rereading it, trying but failing to make the time go by faster. It's an endless loop of looking at the watch on my wrist and tapping my pen against the wooden surface of the desk, and I'm starting to shake with desperation. I need to see him, and I need to do it now.

At long last, it's eleven-thirty, and I change into sweatpants and a soft t-shirt. Something easily accessible. I need him inside me. I need it like I need air in order to stay alive, and lately, I've been no stranger to feeling as if I'm suffocating. At least that's the way I've felt every time he leaves me in the night, going back to wherever it is he goes when he's not with me. I ache for him to be by my side at all times, even though I know it's not smart or possible as long as I stay in this seminary.

Opening my door quietly, I peek my head out and look around. It's dark, save for the light above the stove, and I step out of my room and shut the door so softly it makes no sound. I exhale roughly, my hands shaking as I roam the seminary with hushed steps until I finally make it to the chapel. It's cold and empty, and everything is still. I can hear my ragged breathing as I walk toward the booth, and it's so loud I sound like I'm panting. And maybe I am. It always makes me nervous to sneak around at night to meet up with Azriel. At the same time, I can't not do it. I'd risk it all for him, and I think he knows it at this point.

The door to the confessional booth is open, and I walk closer to it until I see him. Azriel is sitting on the bench, legs spread, and I trail my eyes up the strong muscles of his legs. Up, up, up. Until I focus on the hairless smooth skin of his inner thighs and lose my breath. Then, because I can't help myself, my eyes shift to his balls and cock.

I gasp at the sight before me, feeling like this is all a dream. Like I'll wake up and lose it all—him, my new hopes and dreams. I can't even bear to think about it, and I dig my fingernails into the palms of my hands as I try to ground myself once more and not think of anything but him.

"Come, Elijah," Azriel says softly, one side of his lips tilting up in a soft smirk. "Take your clothes off and get on my lap."

My breathing changes, shallowing once more at his words, and it feels like I'm on the verge of a panic attack. I also feel the calmest I've ever been. Sure of myself for the first time in my life. Sure of what I want. There's no doubt in my mind that it's him. So I take off my sweatpants and shirt, letting them pool at my feet, and step into the booth with him. I climb onto his lap just as he said, kneeling on the bench and shifting my weight so I'm as close to him as possible.

"No underwear then?" Azriel asks with a grin, running his hands up the back of my legs until they rest on my hips. Then, without hesitation, he grabs onto my cheeks and spreads them. I gasp. "Is your hole ready for me?"

I shake my head. "N-no." His finger dips and rubs

over my rim, and all my muscles tighten in anticipation. "I wanted your fingers to open me up."

"Mmmm," Azriel moans, and the cap of the lube bottle opening sounds like a gunshot. "Are you going to be a good boy for me and ride my cock?"

Azriel's wet fingers trace over my hole, then dip inside, one after the other, until there are three impaling me. He pushes them inside slowly. In and out. In and out. Until my eyes cross and it feels as if I'm going crazy.

I groan, "Is that what you want, Az?" My voice is low and breathy, and I don't even sound like me right now. I sound like a very aroused version of myself. Sensual, bold, wanton. "You want me to get on your cock and impale myself on it?"

"Your mouth is filthy, Little Lamb." Azriel chuckles, fingers slipping from inside of me. He directs his cock to my entrance and then presses into my hole. "Who knew you had it in you?"

"I have a lot in me." I moan when he grabs my hips and pushes into me in one thrust, impaling me on his length the exact way I just told him to. "Your c-cock feels so big inside of me."

My toes curl as he lets me adjust to his girth, and he leans his head back against the wall of the booth and stares up into my eyes. Golden orbs that have green in them swirl with desire, and I realize I've never noticed the green before. How have I not noticed?

"If you think it feels big now, just wait until you're bouncing on it," he whispers, smirking. "You'll feel as if I'm splitting you in half."

"Do it," I tell him, grabbing his shoulders and lifting myself up onto my knees, then lowering myself slowly. It feels like I've taken a shot of adrenaline as his cock pushes against my prostate, and I gasp as I lift myself back up. "Oh f-fuck, Azriel. Fuck."

"I love it when you curse for me," he says through gritted teeth, grabbing my hips tightly and thrusting inside of me just as I begin to lower myself again. I throw my head back in pleasure, eyes squeezed shut as I lose myself to it. "My little saint, not so holy anymore, are you? No. I think I've thoroughly defiled you, haven't I?"

"Y-yes," I moan, riding him faster, bouncing harder as I chase my release. My cock bobs up and down as I do, and it feels heavy, ignored.

"I've stained your soul black, and you've loved every single second, haven't you?"

"*Azriel.*"

"Tell me how much you've loved it," he demands. "I want to hear how you'd give yourself over to me—give everything up for me."

"I would," I cry out, feeling myself creeping closer to the edge of the cliff, yet I'm unable to plummet without a hand on my cock. "I'd do whatever you wanted."

"That's right, Little Lamb," he whispers, threading

his fingers through my hair and exposing my throat. He nips at my neck, at my Adam's apple, then licks my skin in one long wet stripe. "I want you to give it all up. Come with me. Leave this all behind."

"Do you mean it?" I whimper, my fingers digging into his shoulders as he bites me hard on the side of my neck.

"I mean everything I say."

"Oh, God. Azriel, please."

"What do you need?" he asks, hands now spreading my cheeks as I fuck myself on his cock.

"Touch my cock please," I beg him. "Make me come."

"Not yet." He grins. "I'm quite enjoying this."

"*Please*," I beg. "Please, I can't take it anymore. I need—" I gasp when he begins to top from the bottom, hitting my prostate over and over like an arrow. "I n-need to—"

"You'll come when I say you can," Azriel growls, fucking me harder. He thrusts two fingers into my mouth and to the back of my throat, and I suck hard. He moans, "There, Beloved. Suck on those for now."

I groan in pleasure as he hits my prostate, and he slides his fingers from between my lips down my chest so slowly I'm shaking in anticipation. And when he finally, finally wraps his hand around my cock and grips it tightly, I sob with relief.

"Y-yes, Azriel. Fuck me. Claim me," I say frantically, thrusting my hips into his fist and slamming my ass back down onto his cock. "Make me your altar."

"Mine," Azriel whispers against my throat, his hand frantic now. My balls tighten and my cock jerks, and intense pleasure floods my body as I come and come and come. "Only mine. Only ever mine."

"Azriel," I moan as the last dribble of cum spurts out of me, and I feel him throb inside of me, coating my insides with the evidence of his pleasure. He cries out as he fills me, and the church bells toll, drowning out the sounds I love so much.

"*Elijah*," he groans, stopping all movements, letting go of my now soft cock. "You were made for me, weren't you?"

"Was I?" I whisper, suddenly feeling shy.

"Yes, Beloved." He nods frantically, searching my eyes. "God made you in my image—not his. He made you just for me."

I somehow believe that. I know it's absolutely insane, but maybe it doesn't need to make sense. I can feel it. I know there's truth to his words.

"I lo—" I begin but am cut off suddenly.

"How sweet," Micah snarls from the open doorway. I hadn't even noticed that I hadn't closed it. Oh, God. "I thought you were better than this, Elijah."

His eyes are focused on where Azriel is still inside of me, and his cheeks heat. But I don't think it's from embarrassment. No, I think it's from rage. From the fact that I've rejected him to be with another man.

"Look away from what's mine, Micah," Azriel growls. "Or I'll gouge your fucking eyes from your skull."

I flinch, but surprisingly, Micah doesn't react at all.

I whimper as I kneel, and Azriel slips out of me, cum trickling out of my hole and down my thighs. I look up to make eye contact with Micah, but he just shakes his head and retreats, a look of pain on his face.

I'm gasping for air, scrambling off Azriel's lap and putting my clothes on in a rush. Azriel calls for me, but I ignore him. I have to stop Micah. He's spiteful—he will talk. I know it. He will tell Father Jacob what he saw, and then I'll be cast out.

Would that really be so bad?

I shake as I run after him, but he's fast. Micah is in the living room by the time I catch up to him, walking quickly towards his room. I grab him by his right arm and yank him back until he's turned around to face me. There are tears streaming down his face, and he sniffles, using his free hand to wipe at his cheeks aggressively. My hand is still wrapped around his bicep, fingers digging in, and he shakes me off.

Taking a step back, I put a few feet of space between us. Micah's green eyes search mine, and my mouth goes dry.

"Micah, I'm s-s-so sorry." I stammer, unsure of

how to act or what to say to make this better. "I didn't mean for you to see that. I didn't want to—"

"To what?" he spits. "Reject me? Break my heart? Too fucking late."

"I've never—"

"Leave him," Micah growls, getting closer to me and wrapping a hand around my neck. "I won't say anything if you leave him and choose me instead."

"I—" I shake my head furiously, tears stinging the back of my eyes. "I can't do that. I won't. He's the love of my life, Micah."

I love him. Oh, fuck. I love Azriel.

"Then you leave me no choice," Micah whispers, letting his hand drop from my neck.

I take in a much-needed breath, and he shakes his head and retreats, stepping backward into the hallway. With one last sad look, he goes to his room and closes the door.

And me?

I fall to my knees and sob.

Terrified.

Chapter 10
Azriel

I haven't seen Elijah in days. Long, lonely, horrible days. I could lie and say I don't know how many days it's been, but I think I've counted the exact hours, minutes, and seconds we've been apart. I don't think—I know. It's become an obsession at this point. Something to do to keep from going crazy, though I'm not sure it's worked. If anything, it has made me feel even crazier.

I knew things would change when I saw Micah standing across from us, but I didn't realize it would be this jarring. That he would give up on us so suddenly. So quickly. As if we never happened. He blew out the candle and walked away, plain and simple. Snuffed out is what we are. There's no better way to describe it. I felt him ripping my heart out the moment he ignored me to run after him, and now there's an Elijah-sized hole in the middle of my chest. It feels raw and painful. Like chunks of me are missing. I never thought I'd feel this again, but here we are. Except this time, it's worse. It hurts *more*.

They're probably together now, and that's why he hasn't come to me. It definitely hasn't been for lack of trying on my part. I've been leaving him notes while he's at evening prayer, hoping he'd come by the chapel in the forest. I've had to be careful not to go see him in the middle of the night. The last thing we need is for Micah to tell on Elijah, and knowing him, he either has already or will at some point. That's why I've kept my distance. I don't want to aggravate the situation with my presence. I don't want to provoke Micah into doing something that will hurt my sweet boy.

It makes me wonder though—are they together? Has Elijah moved on from me that easily? Does he miss me? Why won't he come see me? Has he forgotten me? Does he just not want me anymore? Fuck. I can't take it. I really can't bear it at all. I'm going out of my fucking mind with need for him. I have to see him. I have to.

I've spent the last few days in the chapel ruins in the forest. Every single night I've waited here—all damn night—just in case he decided to show up. Every night, he has let me down. Not only is he gone now, but there is an echo of him living inside of me. A voice that begs, one that sounds exactly like him. Reminding me every day of what I've lost. Taunting me, really.

Please, Azriel. Please touch me. Please touch my cock.

It's driving me insane.

Then there's his voice saying other things. Sweet words. Words I wish had actually come from his lips. Words that put my worries to rest. Ones I know will probably never be spoken now, and it breaks me slowly. There are shards of my heart lying at my feet, and the fissures in my chest will surely never heal. No one will ever fill them up like he has.

I want to scream. Scream at him to come back. And it makes me hate myself a little more with each passing second because—why the fuck didn't I go after him when he ran off? I could've saved myself so much heartache. Or maybe it would be worse actually. To know for sure that he ended things with me. But at least I wouldn't be stuck in this state of limbo. My chest wouldn't be caving in as I wonder where he is. What he's doing. Who he's with.

The worst part is that it doesn't take much imagination to come up with those answers. Surely he's given Micah a chance now, and they're long gone from this shitty place. They've probably started a life far away from here. Meanwhile, I'm stuck. Unable to move on. Fixated on deep blue eyes that saw me clearly, a wide smile I thought was just for me, and sweet little nothings whispered into the dark. I can't stop thinking about any of it.

I'm clearly obsessed.

Certifiable.

I should probably accept that it's over so I can

move on. I just don't know how to. I'm not sure how to put him out of my mind and crawl back into the hole I came out of. He summoned me, but he didn't release me. It's not that I require that, it's that in this case, I wish he had banished me so that I don't get any ideas of sticking around. Because what if I can never get over him? I thought I was in love with Isaac, but he seems insignificant in light of these recent events and how I've reacted. How my body, my soul, my heart have behaved.

It's not that it was easy to get over Isaac. It wasn't. What they did to me, the way they cast me out and scattered his soul shattered me. I thought I'd never recover from it. But the truth is, I did. I was almost whole again when Elijah called out to me. Now, though? I'm ruined, destroyed, annihilated.

There's a dull thud right outside the chapel doors, and I tense, holding my breath to hear more clearly. Except my lungs start to burn, and all I can hear is my heartbeat in my ears. The doors fly open, and in comes Elijah, flustered and out of breath, looking like he hasn't slept in days. My heart soars at seeing the object of my affection so close to me once more, and I walk quickly toward him. Maybe too quickly, because he slams the doors and presses his back to them, eyes wide and mouth agape. We're breathing equally as hard, panting filling the small space of the chapel, and I get closer. I'm aware I should back up a few steps and put some space between us, but it's pointless. There's no way in hell I'll be doing that.

I ignore all the red flags and alarm bells blaring in my mind and step even closer, completely obliterating the space between us and pressing my forehead to his. We're sharing breath, and he tilts his head back and looks into my eyes. I want to scream at him, demand he tell me why he didn't come before now, but instead I'm quiet. Instead I pretend. That I'm sane. That I have my wits about me. It's the furthest thing from the truth, but I don't want to scare him off when I just got him back.

Elijah's bottom lip trembles, and he reaches up to cup my face, making my hands shake just as hard as his are right now. Fuck, how do I do this? How do I ask him if he's betrayed me? I don't know if I can speak—I don't know how to anymore. There's a lump in my throat the size of this country, and I don't think anything will make it better. Short of him coming back to me. Maybe that's why he's here.

Please, let that be why he's here.

His fingers are searing hot when they make contact with my skin, and his hand perfectly curves around my jaw. I bite my bottom lip to keep myself from speaking, instead waiting for him to make the first move. It needs to be him.

"*Baby*," he murmurs.

My muscles relax as I exhale shakily, my hands trembling as they rest limply at my sides. With his free hand, he grabs one of my own and lifts it to his face. I brush my thumb over his bottom lip and grip his chin between my thumb and forefinger. His eyes are intensely blue even in the low lighting. They look absolutely electric as the moon's light caresses his face, and I suck in a sharp breath when he leans in closer. Just as I'm about to speak, he crashes his lips to mine.

It's a kiss filled with desperation, and arousal wraps itself around my limbs, making my cock hard. He runs his hands over the scars on my back where my wings are supposed to be when I'm not in human form, and I moan when his tongue thrusts into my mouth. Both my hands cup his jaw now, tightening slightly when he groans into the kiss. I open my eyes, wanting to see him because I've missed him. I can't not look at him. What I see instead takes my breath away, because his eyes are already open and glittering with tears, staring into mine. I pull away, ragged breaths making my chest heave, and look down at him.

"I'm sorry, Azriel," he rushes out. "I'm so sorry. I swear I wanted to come sooner—"

"Then why didn't you?" I interrupt. "Did you fuck him? Are you with him now?"

"W-what?" Elijah gasps, eyes wide and bottom lip trembling. "No! He wanted me to leave with him. He wants me to choose him. But I didn't—"

"It's only a matter of time, huh?" I ask him harshly. "I knew you'd never choose me. I knew—"

"Azriel," he growls. "I choose *you*. I don't care if Micah tells them. I don't care if they kick me out. But I need to know we're a sure thing. That we'll be together. That you'll be part of my life as my partner—in the light."

I gulp and whisper, "Elijah—" His eyes blink up at me in confusion as I inhale deeply and take a step back. "If you saw me, the real me, you'd be terrified."

"No, I wouldn't," Elijah reassures me, but I shake my head quickly—he would be. "It's you, Azriel. It'll always be you."

"You don't know what you're talking about," I reply softly, unsure of why I'm doing this. I'm happy he's here. That he came back for me. So why am I pushing him away?

"You won't push me away," he says through gritted teeth, reading my mind somehow. "I won't let you."

"You can't—"

"Show me," Elijah says, raising his chin defiantly. "Let me see what's so scary about you."

I shake my head.

"I won't let you leave me." He takes a step forward, grabbing the back of my neck and pressing his lips to mine briefly. It feels like I'm going to plummet into an abyss, and I don't know how to stop myself from taking the plunge. "I won't allow it."

I take a step back and close my eyes, summoning my true form. I feel my wings sprout from my back, spreading wide, and open my eyes. His jaw is slack, and though he's seen them before, I haven't shown him like this. There are shadows dancing around me, yet my skin glows golden. His eyes are transfixed on the ancient symbols carved into my skin.

Anxiety makes my hands shake as he looks at me top to bottom, then his eyes focus on my face. He sucks in a sharp breath, and it terrifies me. I knew I shouldn't have shown him. He's scared. I know it—

"You're so beautiful, Azriel," Elijah says in a hoarse voice. "The most gorgeous man I've ever seen. You're divine."

Divine.

Elijah falls to his knees in front of me, running his warm fingers up the back of my thighs and gripping my ass as he gets closer to me. He doesn't break eye contact. It's surreal, and it makes me tremble as if I've never had anyone on their knees before me. But he's different. He's the only one who's mattered this much.

"Let me worship you, baby," he says softly. "Please. I—I want…"

"Yes, Elijah?" I ask softly. "What do you want?"

"Your cock," he says confidently, and it makes my balls tighten. He raises his chin. "Feed it to me."

"You want me to stuff my cock between those perfect lips and fuck your throat?" I ask him hoarsely, gripping my cock and pressing it to his soft lips. I smear the precum all over the bottom one, and when his tongue makes contact with my slit, I whimper. "Fuck, Elijah."

Elijah nods, parting his lips and directing my cock into his mouth. The first suck is heavenly—absolutely euphoric as he twirls his tongue around the head. His hands tighten on my ass as he pushes me deeper into his mouth, and I bury my fingers in his hair and grip it roughly, thrusting my cock in and out of his mouth. I go as deep as I can, feeling his throat contract around me when I hit the back of it. He gags violently, and I try to pull away slightly, but it only makes him grip me harder.

"Oh, fuck, Eli," I moan loudly, starting to feel a tinge of desperation taking over. "What I feel for you—it's too much, too deep, too fast. But I—I can't help it. I can't stop myself. Please tell me you feel it too," I beg. "Please show me."

Elijah bobs his head faster, taking me deeper somehow. He looks feral as he swallows my cock over and over, and when he reaches around and cradles my balls in his hand, I tense, feeling my impending orgasm rushing to the surface. He squeezes softly, making me gasp, and my hips suddenly have a mind of their own as I pound my cock into his throat. There are tears in his eyes, streaking down his face, and spit coating his chin and my groin, running down my balls now too.

"That's it, my pretty little slut," I groan. "Let me come down your throat. Let me use you as a fuck hole." Elijah moans when I say this to him, and my spine tingles as my balls draw up. "*Yes—*"

Elijah's moans rival my own as I tense and start to come, shooting my load down his throat. His eyes widen as I begin to glow, my skin shining golden as I call out his name, both my hands wrapping around his head as I shove him down on my cock. I come for what feels like forever, and he swallows it all, falling onto his ass when I let go of him. My breathing is labored as I stare down at him, and he's slack-jawed and wide-eyed as I kneel in front of him.

I reach out, tracing my fingers down his cheek and gripping his jaw. Elijah looks wrecked, and right as our lips are about to meet, he whispers, "I love you. Even if it damns me."

My sharp intake of breath is loud as his words echo in my mind, and I shake my head. "Nothing this precious will ever damn you, Elijah," I whisper, caressing his cheek again. "I won't let it."

"A-are you..." Elijah trails off, gulping as I look into his very blue eyes. "Are you in love with me?"

"Of course I am," I reply softly, pressing my lips to his for a moment, then pulling back. "What's not to love?"

Elijah's perfect face contorts into a smile. Full lips stretching wide and narrow nose crinkling with happiness. His almond-shaped blue eyes have fine lines in the corners, and it's just evidence of how I affect him. It stops my heart.

I wish he could see himself the way I see him. If he did, he'd never question his worth again.

Never.

chapter 11
elijah

The chapel is quiet, save for Father Jacob's booming voice as he goes on and on about purity and sin, and it feels oddly directed at me. I'm not trying to be paranoid, but his eyes have gravitated toward me the entire time we've been in mass. I'm sitting at the beginning of the pew, closest to the aisle, hoping that I can make a quick escape once we're done receiving communion and get dismissed. I have a feeling I won't be allowed to go that easily, and my stomach churns at the thought of being singled out again.

Micah has been avoiding me. He won't sit with me anymore or even look my way, and it's bothering me for multiple reasons. For one, I thought we were friends. Good friends. *Best* friends, even. That's clearly done and over with, and I'm pretty sure he spoke to Father Jacob if the evil glint in his eyes is any indication. I want to say I can't believe he'd do that, but he told me he would. When people show you their true colors, you better believe them.

I look over at Micah, who faces forward, unflinching when Father Jacob calls my name. I, however, do flinch. I do it so hard my neck hurts from it, and I exhale roughly when all eyes turn to me. All eyes except for my friend's. The only friend I've ever had. It pisses me off, and I have to breathe in deeply and remind myself I'm not that person. That I'm a man of God. And men of God don't lose their temper.

Wait.

I'm *not* a man of God anymore though. I can't be. Not if the way Father Jacob is sneering at me is any indication. He walks down the aisle and stands a few feet from where I'm sitting, casting a glance around the chapel as if looking for something. Or, rather, someone. Azriel, I realize.

My hands turn clammy, and a shiver runs down my spine at the thought of them doing something to him. I'm not sure what it is they could do, but the thought of him being out of my life forever has my lip curling in a sneer. I won't let them take him away from me. Over my dead body.

"Brother Elijah," Father Jacob says, face hard as stone, eyes narrowing at my facial expression. The one I know I can't disguise anymore, no matter how hard I try. I'm done. "You'd know all about sinning, wouldn't you?"

My head whips to look at Micah, who has his head cocked to the side, and I snarl at him. I've never hated someone before, but I'm pretty sure that's what I'm feeling right now. A deep hatred that's ingrained into my bones. I will fucking kill him.

I stand abruptly, causing Father Jacob to stumble back a step, fear in his eyes for one fleeting second before he masks it once more. But it was there. I didn't imagine it. He's scared of me right now. Of Azriel too. I know it. I can feel it. So I take another step forward until I'm standing in the aisle right across from him. This time, he stands his ground, not wanting to look weak even though he clearly is.

"We are gathered here today because one of our own has fallen, and we must lift him up once again." There are gasps from the other seminarians, and I throw my head back and laugh. Father Jacob's eyes narrow. "He must repent and be made holy once more."

At this, my hands do shake. Mostly because I've tried so hard to escape the shame that eats at me, but he's pressing a button I've tried to disable, and he's pushing and pushing. He must sense my weakness, because his lips curl into an evil grin. I dip my chin, and just as I'm about to make a run for it, I hear footsteps behind me. I'm hauled into a warm body, one I'd recognize anywhere, and gasp. I'm not sure if I feel relieved or terrified. I think both. I can't shield him from this, and I don't like the look in Father Jacob's eyes.

"Come, Elijah," Father Jacob demands, stretching

a hand toward me. "You must remember your place in this church."

"My place is by his side," I reply with my chin raised in defiance, and he bristles.

Father Jacob lifts his hand and makes the sign of the cross over me, then sprinkles me with holy water. I flinch, casting my eyes down, before I remember to be strong and make eye contact again. This time, I'm unmoving and unflinching, letting Azriel's arm around my waist give me strength.

"I command you, demon, whoever you are, attacking this servant of God, depart!" Father Jacob yells, his voice echoing in the chapel.

Azriel laughs, low and throaty. "Elijah is not possessed. He is chosen."

My body relaxes slightly at his words, and this time I smile. My lashes flutter when his hand tightens around my hip, and my cheeks heat. "You call him a demon," I say to Father Jacob, making eye contact with him. He's shaking and red with anger, and it brings me a deep sense of satisfaction. "But he saved me."

"He damned you," Father Jacob spits. "You'll burn in eternal fire—"

"Then I'll burn with him!" I yell. "I promised myself to him. Our souls are bound for all eternity, and if I must burn, then so be it."

Father Jacob's top lip curls as he takes a step forward, and Azriel pulls me into his side immediately, shielding me with a wing around my body. I feel safe. For the first time in my life, I'm right where I belong.

"Leave," Father Jacob says, voice shaking. "You are no longer welcome here. We cast you out, heathen. From now until the end of time, we rebuke you."

I nod, though my entire body is now violently shaking. There are tears in my eyes as I turn around and walk away, going to my room to pack my things. I'm not crying because I'm sad I won't be part of this anymore. I'm crying because I wasted years of my life doing this. Because I gave the church parts of me I'll never get back now.

Azriel follows me into my room as I open the door, and I get my suitcase out of the closet and begin to shove all my belongings in there. I don't have much, which means this will be quick. I'm not sure if I'm grateful for that or if it's making me feel even worse. I can so easily leave this place behind, but it'll always leave me broken and scarred.

"Meet me at the chapel in the woods when you're done here," Azriel says softly, pressing a hand to my lower back as I shove even more clothes into my luggage. "Our place."

"Alright." I nod once, and he leans in and kisses me. He pulls away quickly though, making me miss him immediately.

Azriel leaves quietly as I finish packing, going to my bathroom to get my toothbrush and toiletries.

When I come back into my room, Micah is standing next to my open suitcase and staring at it. I stop in my tracks, not knowing what to do. Before I can decide, he turns around and makes eye contact with me. I want to kick him out, scream at him, and hit him. Instead, I stay quiet and wait for him to get it off his chest. He's clearly here for a reason. But he just stands there and stares, saying nothing.

I walk past him and finish packing, closing the zipper of my luggage and hauling it off the bed. I grab the handle and begin to walk away, but when Micah clears his throat, I stop in my tracks. I don't look at him though, instead, facing forward. I'm halfway out the door anyway, and there's nothing he can say to get me to stay now.

"You should've picked me," Micah whispers, and my hands shake with my restraint. I'm doing my best not to walk back and throttle him, which means I really need to get out of here. Quickly. "It should've been me."

"Thank your God it wasn't," I spit. "I'll never live a lie with you."

"Elijah—"

"Have a nice life," I tell him, cutting him off. "I hope I never see you again."

With those parting words, I leave.

All I feel is relief.

chapter 12
azriel

Elijah looks otherworldly as he lies on his back in the middle of the circle I carved into the tile of the abandoned chapel. His legs are spread, giving me a perfect view of the hole I'm going to fill tonight, cock hard in his hand as he strokes it slowly. His lashes flutter as he stares at me, lids drooping, mouth parted on a moan. The light of the full, yellow moon shines on him, making him look like he belongs in heaven, and suddenly, I feel unworthy of such a perfect man.

He came here right after packing, dragging his luggage and throwing it to the side once he got here. We crashed into each other with so much force that my soul was rearranged, and his clothes were off before I knew what was happening. I'm aware we need to leave the seminary, but I couldn't bring myself to reject him. He wants my body—he said he needed it to feel better. So that's what I'm doing. Once we're done, we can go far away.

I spent hours thinking about what's next for us

after we move on from here. Staying in Texas is out of the question, and we've never had a conversation about the possibilities of our future. I don't think he ever considered leaving the church willingly, and now life is slapping him across the face. He's being forced out, just as he always feared. Nonetheless, I will remain by his side through it all. We just need to figure out our next steps. I refuse to go blindly.

Kneeling between his thighs, I watch in amazement as he fingers lube into his hole. Two fingers thrust in and out of him, and I press one of mine to his entrance to add a third. The moan he lets out is the most erotic sound I've ever heard, making my cock jerk against my abs.

"You're beautiful," I murmur, thrusting my finger in deeper until he mewls, his entire body squirming with pleasure. "Are you mine, Elijah?"

"Yes," he says quickly. "All yours."

A smile tips my lips as I pull our fingers out of his body and fist my cock, covering it with lube and pressing it to his entrance. I watch, mesmerized, as Elijah's chest heaves. His breaths are shallow and loud, and a shiver runs down my spine in anticipation. I push forward, the head of my cock is suddenly enveloped in tight heat, and his eyes blaze with lust.

"Tell me you're mine too," Elijah demands. "Show me you're my forever. My always."

"I'm going to show you every day for the rest of our lives," I reply reverently, pushing in deeper. He hisses, wrapping his legs around my waist as I bottom out, thrusting roughly into him once. "Oh, for fuck's sake, Elijah. This ass was made for me."

"*Yes.*" He nods rapidly as I pull back and thrust forward hard enough to have him sliding up on the tile. "Fuck me harder."

I do, thrusting harder into him, harder than I ever have. His eyes roll to the back of his head as I hit his prostate, his body curling into me, and his lips latching onto my chest. I feel him sucking, bruising, and a primal urge to mark him takes over when I wrap a hand around his throat and push him away. His head meets the tile once more, back arching, and he exposes his throat for me just as I want him to. It's as if he can read my mind.

My lips find purchase on his neck as I lick, suck, and bite him. He moans and mewls under me, making animalistic sounds I've never heard from him before. It spurs me on, and I wrap a hand around his length as I piston my hips into that sweet little spot inside of him. Elijah's body shakes, then tightens, as his release is about to hit him.

I let go and pull out.

"No, no, *no.*" He shakes his head vehemently. "W-what the hell are you doing, Azriel? Make me come!"

"Needy," I chuckle. "You'll come when I let you."

Elijah looks desperate as he continues to shake his head, then grabs my hair and pushes me down onto his cock. I oblige him, taking him deep into my mouth until he's in the back of my throat. I hold him there, nose pressed to his base as I breathe in through my nose and fight the gag reflex trying to take over. I slip three fingers into his sloppy hole, crooking them and finding his prostate once more.

I'm about to pull away and edge him once more when he wraps his thighs around my neck and fucks into my mouth roughly, his cock hitting the back of my throat repeatedly. It's the sexiest thing he's ever done, hands down.

"*Azriel,*" Elijah groans, and I get a stream of precum in my mouth. I swallow it greedily as I push harder against his prostate, and his fingers tighten in my hair until there are tears streaming down my face. "You look like an angel with my cock in your mouth, baby. Like my angel."

I hum.

"Relax your jaw," he says soothingly. "Let me fuck your throat. I want you to feel me for days. I want you to remember who you belong to. The only one you'll *ever* belong to. It's me. Us. Forever."

His breathing is ragged as he speaks, fucking my throat harder, making me gag with every thrust. My nostrils flare in an attempt to keep my composure, and I fuck him with my fingers a little faster.

"Yes, yes, *yes*." Elijah chants. "More. More. Please, Azriel. Fuck me faster! Harder."

Fuck.

There's no way I'm going to last once he's done. I

need to be in his hole, and I need to be in it now. Right fucking now. I can't wait any longer. With one more crook of my fingers he tenses, gritting his teeth.

"Finger your hole, Az," he demands, now fisting my hair with both hands as he fucks into my mouth. "I want to slide in that tight ass tonight."

I moan, then lube up my fingers quickly, my other hand busy working him open. I'm kneeling awkwardly between Elijah's legs, but he's keeping me up using my hair like reins as he rides my mouth. I add two fingers into my hole, and just as I pull them out, he throws his head back and screams.

"Oh, fuck! Oh, God," he says, making my stomach tingle and flip. "I love you. Oh, fuck, Azriel, I love you so much."

With those final words, his cum hits the back of my throat. His thrusts are relentless, and even though I try to swallow it all, his cum still slips down my chin and onto my neck. When he pulls out of my mouth, it's game over. I remove my fingers from his body and grasp his hips, pulling him toward me. And then I flip him.

Elijah's now on his hands and knees, and I shove his head down until his cheek meets the tile, his arms bending until he's bracing himself on his forearms. His ass is muscular and round, making my mouth water, but I'm too desperate to be inside of him right now. I'll taste him later.

I lube up once more and thrust into him,

bottoming out and pulling my hips back immediately. I moan at the sensation of his heat enveloping my cock, and I use the back of his neck as leverage as I begin to fuck him in earnest. My body drapes over his, my chest to his back, and I curl my body over his as I bite his earlobe.

"Elijah," I growl. "I've never—" Gasping, I squeeze my eyes shut. "I've never felt like this about anyone before."

"No?" he asks, out of breath. "Not even with…"

"No," I admit. "Just you. Oh, fuck, Eli. Touch your cock."

"I don't want to come again yet," he whines. "I'm going to come in your hole tonight. I'm going to make you filthy and mine."

"I'm already yours," I tell him, fucking him faster and harder. I wrap an arm around his waist and pull him up to me so he's kneeling on top of me, ass slapping my thighs as I fuck into him. "Shit. Fuck."

"Is that all you got, Azriel?" Elijah taunts, and I can hear the smirk in his voice. "Won't you give me more?"

Grabbing his hips, I fuck him harder and faster, and his hole tightens around me. He's not touching his cock yet, and I know he wants me to come inside of him so we can flip. He wants to mark me tonight. And I'm ready to give this part of me over to him.

My wings tremble violently with my pleasure, something I've never felt before, and I bury myself into his neck and groan. "Saint, sinner, lover, lamb," I whisper against his skin, and he moans. "Mine, mine, all fucking *mine*."

I come with a growl, burying my cock as deep as it'll go. I fuck him through my orgasm, hoping it pushes him closer to his. I want to feel him drip out of me, and I want it right now.

Elijah lifts himself off my cock and turns around, pushing me down onto the tile until I'm lying on my back. He spreads my legs, urging me to hold them for him, as he slathers lube on his cock and presses it to my entrance. He's gentle as the head of his cock slips into my hole, a burning sensation gripping me when he pushes through the ring of muscle. He thrusts into me softly, slowly, and I accidentally shut my eyes when he bottoms out.

"Eyes on me, Az," Elijah demands. "You need to see who's fucking you tonight. The only man who will be fucking you for the rest of your days."

"Swear it," I growl. "Swear it'll be forever."

Elijah's features are tight, and he's clearly holding back. "I swear it." He runs a hand down my chest and abs until it wraps around my half-hard cock, and I shiver at how sensitive it feels. He tugs on it, making it harden once more, and begins to move slowly.

His hips roll sensually, and I watch in awe as he absolutely fucking glows. My thighs wrap around his hips as he goes deeper, hitting my prostate, and my back bows off the ground. I throw my head back and groan, panting, and he does it over and over again. We're both wordless and sputtering for breath, and this just feels like more. More than fucking. This feels like I'm giving him a piece of me I've never handed over before.

"Elijah," I gasp. "You fuck me so good. Please don't stop. Please right there—"

"Here?"

"Yes, yes!" I moan loudly as he hits my prostate once more. "Please."

"What are you begging for?" he asks, jerking my cock fast and hard as he fucks me. "You want me to paint you with my cum, Azriel? Claim you once and for all? Make you mine?"

"Yes." I nod, my hands roaming down his back and grabbing his ass as I push him deeper into me. "All of that. Give me everything. I want it all."

My spine begins to tingle the longer he works my body like an instrument, and it feels like all my strings are about to snap. The room begins to glow, starting from the symbols carved into the tile. It's a golden light rising from the ground up, wrapping around Elijah and I as he goes faster. He looks around in awe, mouth agape, and he hits my prostate again, causing my body to tighten with my release.

Cum explodes out of my cock as I rock my hips into him and chase friction. My orgasm goes on for what feels like forever, and Elijah's hand wraps around my throat tightly as he comes inside of me. I feel his cock throb and liquid heat fill my insides, but what actually makes me feel powerful is the way he looks. Wrecked. Absolutely unraveled. When he makes eye contact with me, his fingers flex on my neck, and he shudders.

Something happened between us tonight.

Something...*more*.

That's undeniable.

It cements everything I've believed to be true—that this is the right choice for both of us. That we belong together and to each other. That nothing and no one will tear us apart.

Not now.

Not ever.

epilogue
elijah

A YEAR LATER...

The bell above the door chimes when Azriel comes into our shop, and I smile at him widely as I put the lady's items in a bag and hand them to her. I tell her to have a good day, and she tells me to do the same. She looks around at the eclectic decor one more time before she heads for the door and leaves, and I grin. I love it here. Owning a shop selling banned books, candles, and charms in the French Quarter in New Orleans is not what I thought I'd be doing with my life, but I wouldn't trade it for the world.

Having the freedom to live my life as I choose, to love who I love, is a gift I never thought I'd receive. And I owe it all to Azriel, the love of my life. He's walked alongside me in human skin for a year now, only letting his wings come out in our home, where no one can see him. I've loved every second of seeing him come out of his shell and discovering who he is as a person, and I'm sure he's loved every second of seeing me do the same. We're learning and growing together, walking this life side by side with fingers interlaced. We're *living*.

Living has never felt so good, and the seminary closing in Texas has just been the cherry on top. No one knows how or why it happened, but I have a sneaking suspicion it's thanks to Azriel. He'll never admit to it though, and I don't care enough about that place to pressure him. I'm just happy it's over. That we're out of there, and that no more people will get hurt because of that cult. Because that's what it is, a cult. I don't believe in religion anymore, and the God I believed in all my life is a God of punishment, not love. Now, my beliefs have shifted. I believe in what Azriel gives me every day—his heart, his soul, his everything. That's all I need, all I'll ever need.

I watch as Azriel shuts the door and locks it, flipping the sign from open to closed. He turns around with a grin on his face, and I raise an eyebrow. We're not supposed to close for another two hours, so whatever he has planned better be good. Though I truly don't mind spending every waking moment by his side, no matter what we're doing.

He makes his way towards me, offering his hand when he finally stops a few feet across from me. I walk to him and take it, and he leans in and gives me a soft kiss on the lips, then drags me to the back of the store where the stairs lead to our apartment on the second story. We live in the heart of the French Quarter, and while the place is not big by any means, it works for us. My favorite part of the apartment has to be the balcony overlooking the streets of New Orleans. I live for the people watching.

Azriel stops abruptly before opening the door, telling me to cover my eyes. I think about peeking, but I kind of want to be surprised more, so I cover my eyes and shut them tightly, letting him lead me in by my arm. I hear the door shut, and then he's gently guiding me around the living room. I feel the breeze of the chilly October night as he leads me onto the balcony, and when he tells me to open my eyes, I gasp.

There's a covered meal on the small two-seater table on our balcony, and he pulls out a chair for me. I look around at the candles on the floor, and I rack my brain, trying to remember the special occasion when it finally clicks. It's our anniversary. The day of his summoning. I grin at him as I sit, and he lifts the lids off our food. It smells amazing, and it's my favorite—gumbo. He's been patient with me as I learn how to cook for us, but I can't deny, I'm not very motivated when he's so good at putting recipes together.

Sitting across from me, he grins back, and I clean the plate fairly quickly. I make conversation about the shop and the customers, reveling in how easy it is between us. We've adjusted to partnership effortlessly, and I sigh with happiness as I reach for his hand, just to frown when I find it shaking in my grip.

"What's wrong?" I ask Azriel, and he gulps. "Baby?"

His golden eyes are leaning more toward an amber color in his human form, and they're wide right now as he bites on his full bottom lip. I take a long look at his strong nose, chiseled jaw, and brown hair glowing lighter as the sunset casts its beautiful light upon him. I'm hypnotized. Absolutely unable to look away from him.

Azriel lets go of my hand, pushing his chair back and standing. He takes a deep breath and comes to my side, then drops to one knee and looks up at me. I gasp, covering my mouth as his eyes water.

"*Elijah.*" His voice breaks on my name, and a tear spills down my cheek. "From the moment I saw you for the first time, I knew you'd be important to me. I just never realized you'd end up being my treasure, my love, my whole world. I've never loved anyone the way I love you, Beloved, and I'll never love anyone else. You're my reason—my reason to exist. I want to walk beside you for all of eternity, and I want you tied to me in all ways possible."

I watch as tears spill down his cheeks, and my bottom lip wobbles as I sniff. He reaches into his back pocket and produces a simple dark gray band, and when he turns it and the light hits it, I see the engraving on the inside.

Little Lamb.

"Elijah Rivers." He smiles at me, and my heart squeezes in my chest. "Will you do me the honor of being by my side forever? Will you marry me?"

I gasp even though I knew it was coming, and then I smile through my tears and nod quickly, shoving my hand toward him.

Azriel chuckles. "Say it, Little Lamb," he whispers, taking my hand in his and kissing my knuckles. "I want you to say it."

"Yes," I choke out. "I'll spend forever by your side."

The grin on his face is blinding, and he slips the ring onto my finger and kisses it too. It fits perfectly, just the way he does in my life. And yeah, I know forever is a long time by his side, but apparently, I became immortal the moment he bound me to him. So forever really is what I will give him.

Grabbing the back of his head, I pull him to me, pressing my lips to his softly. It quickly grows heated, and he stands, pulling me up with him. I stumble forward into the apartment, but as soon as we make it to the living room, he picks me up and carries me to bed. I bounce when I land on the mattress, looking up at him through my lashes. His cheeks are pink, and I can't tell if it's from the cold, arousal, or his crying. But it makes him look gorgeous.

I want him so badly.

I quickly shed my clothing, and so does he, and when I'm completely bare, I spread my legs for him.

He crawls toward me, hard cock hanging heavily between his thighs as he settles himself between mine, and then he puts my legs over his shoulders and kisses my belly button. It ignites a fire within me, and it doesn't matter that we've done this hundreds of times; it still feels like the first time. He takes me nightly, sometimes soft, sometimes rough, but *always* worshipful.

I moan when his mouth wraps around me, the heat of his tongue circling the head of my cock, making my eyes roll to the back of my head. My hips have a mind of their own as I chase my release, and when I find it, spilling my cum down his throat, I'm reminded of something I've been thinking about every day for the past year.

Azriel was never my demon.

He was the answer to all my prayers.

I plan on living my life just as I was meant to.

By his side.

Forever.

what's next?

Thank you so much for reading Meant to Burn! Please don't forget to review if you enjoyed the book. Reviews are so important to indie authors like me. I am forever grateful for your support!

If you'd like to be part of the community and talk about the book, join the Facebook Group, Ruby's Darklings.

Stalk Me:
My website is **authorshaeruby.com**
Sign up for my newsletter at
authorshaeruby.com/newsletter
Follow me on Facebook at
Facebook.com/authorshaeruby
Join my Reader Group at
Facebook.com/groups/rubysdarkling
Follow me on Instagram, TikTok, and Pinterest:
@authorshaeruby

acknowledgments

Thank you to everyone who has ever supported me. I couldn't do this without you!

To my readers, first and foremost. I want to thank each and every one of you for your love and support.

To my husband, Conner, you're my everything. I love you.

To my mother, thank you for always believing in me. I love you.

To my dad, thank you for always listening to my crazy ideas. I love you!

To Quirky Circe, thank you for always designing the most beautiful covers and interiors!

To Angie, the past three years by your side have been the easiest of my life. Thank you for believing in me.

To Katie Cadwallader, it was love at first sight. You are amazingly talented!

To my beta readers—Ellie, Brittany, Tahlia. I wouldn't be able to do this without you!! I love y'all.

Ellie, my girl. Thank you for sticking by my side

for so many years. I'll never take you for granted. I love you.

Brittany, my ride or die! Love you girl!!!

To my Street Team, you guys are AMAZING!! Thank you for all your help. Wow, I really couldn't do this without every single one of you.

Lastly, I want to thank my social media followers both on Instagram and TikTok, my Facebook page, and my Readers Group. None of this would be possible without you spreading the word about my books!

All of you mean everything to me.

With love,
Shae Ruby

about shae ruby

Author of dark romance & toxic love.

Sometimes diverse.

International Bestselling Author in five different countries, Shae Ruby spends their time writing (mostly queer) books that make you *feel*.

Their stories come from deep within their bleeding heart, and they let the drops flow into their words.

Shae Ruby is represented by Lunar Literary Agency.

For all subsidiary rights, please contact Angie Ojeda-Hazen:

angie@lunarliteraryagency.com

also by shae ruby

THE BROKEN SERIES:

Shattered Hearts (MF)

Battered Souls (Love Triangle)

Tattered Bodies (MFM)

HEATHENS SERIES:

Unhallowed (MMF)

Unholy (MM) — *Coming 2026*

LA FAMIGLIA COLOMBO SERIES:

Shot For Mercy (MM)

Crimson Pact (MM) — *Coming 2026*

STANDALONES:

Bloody Tainted Lies (MF)

Stay With Me (MF)

Antidote (MM)

Cross My Heart (MM)

Summoned (MM)

Meant to Burn (MM)

Before I Lost You (MM) — *Coming Spring 2026*

Printed in Dunstable, United Kingdom